SUMMARY

January 1925.

Violet Carlyle is in the midst of wedding preparations, somehow balancing her stepmother's snobbery with her own wants. Since Lady Eleanor arrived in London, Vi's beloved Jack has thrown himself into case after case.

Out of sheer boredom, Violet accepts an invitation to attend the Piccadilly Ladies Club. When she makes new friends at the club, Violet accepts an invitation for a party. She little expects to stumble upon a body over an evening of cocktails and conversation. Together, Jack and Violet step into the investigation, determined to discover why this woman was murdered and if anyone else is at risk.

MURDER AT THE LADIES CLUB

THE VIOLET CARLYLE MYSTERIES

BETH BYERS

CHAPTER 1

"*L*ady Eleanor," Violet said carefully, trying to hide her growing fury. "No."

Vi had been dressed and ready to leave when her stepmother arrived and pushed her way through the door, despite the butler trying to dissuade her. Lady Eleanor, of course, further ignored the fact that Violet had a car waiting and took a place on the Chesterfield in the parlor, leaning back to tell Violet her plan.

Violet wore her coat as her stepmother spoke in a silent battle of wills. When the explanation was completed, Violet's gaze narrowed, but Lady Eleanor was undeterred.

"You realize he's a duke." Lady Eleanor glanced around the parlor while Violet tried to pull her mouth closed. *Was she mad?*

"No," Violet repeated, precisely, shooting for an even tone and failing. "I don't care who he is. Duke or not, he's both awful and not our friend."

"I'm not accepting a no on this." Lady Eleanor smiled smoothly and evenly, as though she had a right to control Violet's wedding—or for that matter—her life. Her stepmother had already switched Violet's order of peonies to lilies and changed the time of the wedding from the afternoon to the morning.

"He's awful," Violet repeated. "And Jack has never met this *duke*."

"Don't be smart."

"I am not being *smart*," Violet ground out. "Jack's best man will be Hamilton Barnes with Denny and Victor standing up alongside."

"*Barnes*," Lady Eleanor said with a sneer, "is a detective."

"Lady Eleanor," Violet snapped, losing all patience, "so is Jack."

"Well, for now—"

Violet's gaze widened and flicked over her stepmother. Oh by Jove! The woman intended to move her games from Victor and Violet to Jack. Violet was not going to allow it. "You will leave Jack alone."

"Darling, I am focused on what is best for our family—for *your* family. I would think you'd appreciate the sacrifices I make for us all."

Violet rose, adjusted the belt around her coat, and then—while looking down at her stepmother—said, "Jack will not have this man, regardless of his title or status, stand up with him on our wedding day. This is *my* wedding, and you will leave Jack and his friendships and his career alone, or I will start publishing under Lady Violet Carlyle instead of V. V. Twinnings, and you will find a character who is a disturbing mix of you and a vampire and a sewer creature. I will then call up that Emily Allen and invite her to write an article all about my new book. I'm sure she'll make it salacious and awful."

"If you think your father—"

Violet stopped at the doorway and turned back. "If you think my father hasn't realized your games or if you think that I will success-fully let you play them in my marriage, you are very, very wrong. Accept your defeat now."

"Or what?" Lady Eleanor smiled calmly and lifted her brow. She also, however, avoided meeting Violet's gaze.

Violet's head tilted and she smiled slowly, evilly. "Do you truly wish to find out? I can assure you it will be worse than frogs in your bed or whatever other nonsense Victor and I have done to you in the past."

"What I want is for you to acknowledge *who* you are and embrace it. Call off this farce of a marriage and help our family avoid the stigma of a divorce. We all know where it will end, Violet. Stop being a romantic *fool.*"

Violet glared, and she slammed the door of the parlor, snapping at Hargreaves. "Ignore her until she goes away, unless you find her stealing the silver. If she asks for tea or sandwiches, agree and fail to deliver."

Hargreaves was expressionless as Violet took her handbag from the table in the hall and ran down the steps of the house to the waiting car.

"Drive to the grey stone house on the corner and pause for a few minutes," she told the cabbie. "After which, I'll give you the address of where we're actually going."

The driver glanced at Violet. "Whatever you want, lady."

The grey stone house with the wrought iron fence was one of the largest on the street. The window over the door was a stained glass of a night sky. Violet had made her first mark on the house by replacing the gate. The previous gate had rusted, and she had chosen a new wrought iron one, the center of which had been twisted into a dragon form. Jack had laughed when Violet told him what she'd ordered, which told her he was the perfect man for her. She'd ordered dragon-shaped door knockers as well so they'd match. She'd also replaced the stone lions with stone dragons. They were ridiculous and made her smile.

The garden had become overgrown. The gentleman that had owned the house before had been elderly and eventually he'd had to sell. Violet and Jack had the chance to fix everything with their own touches. They'd gone less 'bright young thing' and more 'responsible upper class privileged' with the new paper and art deco touches throughout the stately mansion.

With a new carved bed here, new Chesterfields there, a dining room full of painted, dragon-embossed wall paper, the house was becoming their own. Violet wanted more than anything to move in, which surprised her, since the idea of not living with her twin made her feel lost. Yet somehow, the closer her wedding day came, the more

Victor's London house felt foreign while the home she was creating with Jack felt like where she *should* be.

Violet arrived at Lila's house soon after she left her new home. She had only needed to see it and remember what was ahead. It would help her get through the madness of her stepmother inserting herself back into Vi's life.

"Are you ready?" Lila asked, as she swung the door open. Her long-suffering butler stood behind her. He was not as much of a master of expressionlessness as Hargreaves, so Violet caught his gaze shooting to the ceiling before he tried and failed to smooth it into stone.

Violet winked at the butler and then hooked her arm through Lila's. "Ready to shop for the honeymoon? No." She could feel her face heat thoroughly. "Need to? Yes. I suppose a flannel nightgown to my neck and down to my ankles is out of the question."

"Vi," Lila laughed lazily, "who knew you'd be such a delicate flower? Although—" Lila's voice dropped to a whisper. "I doubt Jack will mind anything you wear."

Violet's face was so hot, she had a hard time thinking beyond the fire in her cheeks. She adjusted the belt of her coat, smoothed her fringe off of her face and asked, "Shall we go?"

THE FABRIC WAS BORDERED with lace and embroidery, but the vast majority of it, if you could use the word 'majority,' was utterly sheer. The—ah, what did you even call something so small? Whatever the name—it would show at least half of her breasts and barely end below her bottom.

Violet slipped her fingers between the slight layers of fabric and noted the outline of her fingers. If she wore this with nothing else beneath it, every single inch of her body would be on display.

"Yes," Lila said instantly. Violet's face heated to a whole other extent. It was painful.

"I—"

"Yes," Lila repeated. "You must. I don't actually want to see the look on Jack's face, but I would very much like to see the look on Denny's if I buy this pink one. Darling, of course with your name, you're buying purple. You have time to order one with violets embroidered along the edges."

"It's just so—"

"Scandalous?"

"Yes!"

"You're getting married, darling. Just because you and Jack are toeing the Victorian line doesn't mean that you aren't going to enjoy what comes next."

Violet shot Lila an entirely useless quelling look. Lila simply laughed. Vi's gaze narrowed. "Are you and Denny still thinking of having children?"

"I—oh! You *are* evil." Lila's grin declared Violet the winner.

"Will you help me find some pretty things and maybe something I won't be too shy to wear at first?"

"Darling," Lila said, cupping Violet's cheek as Jack did so often, "you could wear a burlap sack tied off with ancient mariner rope, and Jack wouldn't even notice. He's so besotted with you all he can see are the stars in your eyes."

Violet shot Lila another quelling look, and her friend merely shrugged. They both paused as another woman came into the boutique. She was, perhaps, a year or two older than Lila and Denny. Exotic with just enough detailing in her wardrobe to show she had bought it somewhere else. Somewhere far and wonderful. Her face was overly brown for the current fashion, but her perfect rouge and lipstick, expensive shoes, with fitted, tailored clothes, those proclaimed that despite her brown skin, she was another of that privileged class that Violet had been thinking of earlier.

Her hair was a golden blonde pulled back into a tight bun, and she had brilliantly blue eyes. She had a straight perfect nose, straight white teeth, and delicate arches to her brows. She was, in many ways, the personification of a typical English woman.

Lila grinned and demanded in her lazy, nosy way, "Where have you been? My goodness! You look like you've just escaped the plains of Africa."

"Does Africa have plains?" Violet asked with a sniff. "I honestly don't know. I suppose that makes me a bit of an idiot. I feel like all I might know about Africa is out of the Tarzan novels. I wonder if those are accurate."

"A little bit of an idiot," the blonde girl said with a giant grin. "Africa is one of the continents, you know? They have plains and mountains and everything."

"Everything?" Lila asked, sounding bored.

"I've just never been." Violet took a long deep breath in and then her gaze turned to Lila.

"No."

"It would be fun."

"No," Lila repeated. "I prefer my vacation spots to have an ocean."

"Africa has oceans," the woman said. She held out a hand to Violet. "If you need a partner for Africa, I am your girl. Rita Russell, darling. It's lovely to meet you."

"Violet Carlyle," Vi replied. "This flower over here is Lila Lancaster. However, I'm about to get a new partner, I'm afraid. Who, I'm sure, would insist on coming with me to Africa."

"Violet Carlyle? *Lady* Violet Carlyle? Lady Violet Carlyle, the author? With her twin, the author V.V. Twinnings? Engaged to the clever Jack Wakefield? That Violet Carlyle?"

Violet glanced at Lila, who had lost her lazy, bored look for shock.

"Why would you know all of that?" Vi demanded.

"Oh," Rita grinned. "I went to school with Emily Allen. Miss Allen, you know, was quite fond of Mr. Wakefield once."

"I am aware," Violet told Rita calmly.

It was Lila who broke the sudden tension with a hysterical giggle. "Your face! Oh my goodness, your face, Violet. It's the pretty version of what Jack looks like when Theodophilus come around. Sort of terrifying and—"

"You know," Rita cut in, "if you're going to so *rudely* abandon me on my next trip to Africa, you simply *must* have tea with me. Or luncheon. Or perhaps we could do both with a long walk in between." Her voice was dry and the way she emphasized her words told Violet that Rita was quietly evil. Violet enjoyed the other woman immediately.

"Oooh," Lila said lazily, "that does sound like quite the commitment for new friends. Perhaps tea, and we'll see where it goes from there."

Violet's laughter of agreement was answer enough, and Rita Russell held out her card. "Tomorrow?"

"So quickly," Lila mused to Violet. "Miss Russell is enchanted with you. I wonder—is it because Emily Allen doesn't like you—"

"Despises her with a fiery passion," Rita inserted. "Let's not water things down."

Lila nodded. "Or is this quick-witted woman entranced because you're an earl's daughter?"

"It was the Africa joke," Rita Russell replied. "If Lady Violet Carlyle didn't know that Africa has plains, mountains, and oceans, I will eat my hat. Therefore, she was playing games with the idiocy of the common bright young thing. I do enjoy a secret joke."

"Oh, I like her," Lila declared. "If I were a lesser woman, I would be more territorial of my friend, but I know my worth. Also," she added to Vi, "she'll like me better than you in the end."

Violet rolled her eyes and took the card Rita held out.

"Oh," Rita told Lila, "you *are* invited too. The infamous Lady Violet Carlyle's dearest friend? What secrets do you hide, my dear?"

"All of them." Lila handed Violet the sheer purple lingerie. "Finish up darling. The big day *is* coming."

Vi took it with a wince, winked at Rita, and then pulled the shop girl into a corner. "Just send over an excessive amount of these types of things."

"The lingerie?" The girl's eyes were wide, and she was biting her bottom lip to hide a wide grin.

"I'll send back what I don't want. I can't possibly, ah, do this with an audience."

"Don't worry," Lila said loudly, "she'll keep it all. Think of the commission." Her comment was followed by a whispered aside to Rita, probably teasing Violet and explaining her as well. Which was confirmed a moment later when Rita Russell's laughter chased Violet out of the boutique.

CHAPTER 2

*V*ictor plopped onto the Chesterfield next to Violet, propped his feet up on the ottoman in front of them and moaned. When Violet didn't react, he moaned again. She lifted a brow his way and then closed her eyes again.

"I had luncheon with Stepmother. Kate somehow was too ill to attend. My twin did not deign to appear."

Vi ignored the twin comment. "Kate seems better lately. I thought the sicking up had stopped. She's—what's the word—glowing?"

Victor grinned, telling Violet without words that Kate had decided that her feet up, a book in her hand, and a box of chocolates was a better option for an afternoon than a meal with her in-law. Victor continued. "Somehow Stepmother seemed to think you were going to be there."

"I wonder why she'd think a foolish thing," Violet mused. "You know, after our little tête-à-tête yesterday, I decided some distance between Lady Eleanor and myself would be a good thing. Perhaps a continent, two."

"She wants to know how to get Jack to stop working. Or, conversely, how to get him to work so much that you'll grow frustrated and leave him. Forever. Perhaps with a long journey on the continent with a rich Russian prince or a poor English duke. She seems to think that you succumbing to a moderately anti-heroic but titled man is romantic. She says your upright morality and idiotic righteousness will redeem this fictional villain."

"It's interesting, isn't it, how the lack of money doesn't matter for someone like His Grace, Duke of the Empty Coffers."

"It's certainly telling, Violet darling. What shall we do about her?"

"I started a new story," she told him. "Just this morning."

"Did you? The one we were talking about?"

"Indeed. I would have loved to be scolded by our stepmother once again, but Jack has been called to Leeds for some case there, and I am avoiding another round of the blues. Especially with you and Kate abandoning me as well. One must be careful."

Victor tossed her an irritated glance. "You are referring to seeing the three houses your man of business found for us in the same neighborhood as Jack's country house?"

"Yes. Abandoning me. It's not like you aren't planning on staying there soon and leaving me here."

"Violet Carlyle, twin, devil, I experienced a half hour-long tirade about the location of the country house we were purchasing in comparison to the country house of my in-laws. Choosing you over Mrs. Lancaster has put me permanently in the doghouse."

"I thought you were buying a house there as well."

"I am," he snapped. "I'm not fully mad! Only, Kate told me we can't go there when she has the baby. Somehow *Mother* has discovered we intend to go to the country house before the baby is born. It's left me as the villain of that side of the family since it cannot possibly be Kate's choice."

Violet's laugh had Victor folding his arms across his chest and gritting his teeth.

"Try not to pout, darling. These are the consequences of combining families. Surely Kate and Violet Junior are worth this terrible sacrifice?"

"Quit mocking me, devil," Victor whined.

Violet elbowed him and then rose. "I'd love to listen to you bemoan your fate for the rest of the afternoon, dear brother, but I have been invited to tea with someone who knows Miss Allen."

"Miss Allen? Of the lesser twin article?"

"Jack's former fiancé? Yes."

Victor winced, and Violet grinned and rose. "Keep me in your thoughts, lesser twin."

Violet ran up the stairs to her bedroom to change. She decided to wash her face and run a brush over her hair before she considered her options. It was January, so a pale pink day dress felt out of season. With her dark hair and eyes, the deep—nearly tan—cream dresses did look particularly nice on Violet.

She pulled that dress out of her armoire, dressed quickly and then carefully applied her makeup, drawing in her brows, blending in her rouge, and darkening her lashes. A moment later and she'd applied her lipstick and placed it in her handbag.

Violet examined herself in the mirror and grinned at the realization she was more worried about how she looked for this tea with Rita Russell—a complete stranger—than she would be if she was dressing to meet Jack for one of those fun little restaurants he hunted up. The thought of Jack made her miss him, and while she kept her grin, it faded to a sort of stalwart grimace.

She hurried down the stairs, adding a dark brown cloche in the hall, and then stuck her head into Victor's office. "It's all your fault."

"It usually is," he said, waiting.

"You've taught me to be dependent. Enabled it."

Victor laughed out and out at that. "Your blues aren't because Jack is working," Victor told her. "You are the least dependent woman in the whole of the world. You run business interests that churn out bullion by the bucket. You know how to operate an automobile, plan trips across the world without a fear or the need of a masculine hand. Darling, you just struggle. It's rather like—ah, people who have gout. Sometimes it's hard for you to be merry. The only thing that I or Lila or Jack do is give you a reason to get out, which always helps. You know what else helps?"

"What?"

"Sunny days. I declare. We should spend every January and February elsewhere. The Riviera. Crete. Barbados. Cuba, again. By Jove! Cuba." The second time he said 'Cuba,' he said it longingly.

"You'll have a baby next time," she told him, suddenly feeling better.

"I'm sure Vi junior will love traveling. Start them young, you know? Begin as you mean to go on."

Violet grinned and dropped a kiss on her brother's forehead. "You do make me feel better."

LILA ARRIVED in a black cab just as Violet left the house. She had thought she'd wander past the house she and Jack had purchased, but Lila had arrived too early to let Violet dream over her house a little more.

"Oh my goodness," Lila said, crossing her legs, "are you mooning over your house again? It's yours now, Vi. By Jove, woman! Move in, have a party."

"A party." Violet grinned slowly. "We do need to add our own particular flavor to the house."

"Before we get there," Lila mused, "do you wonder if that Russell woman somehow knew we would be in that particular boutique?"

"It is odd, isn't it?" Vi mused in return, imitating Lila's tone. "There is no way, darling one. We didn't know we'd be at that boutique when we left."

"They could have guessed," Lila said. "It's not like we aren't pretty—what's the word? Reliable? Devoted? Addicted? That might be it. To several particular boutiques and shops. You keep Ursula Grant's shop in business, I think."

"Her embroiderers do divine work. I like this idea of a party."

"So you're going to ignore my question?"

"I am!" Violet grinned, then tilted her head as she examined Lila. The woman was—like Violet—twenty-four-years-old. They had been the best of friends since their first day of boarding school when Violet had been lost without Victor and Lila had been lost without her best friend, Denny.

So much had changed since then, but occasionally, Violet felt as though she could see the tiny versions of them. As much as Vi loved her sister Isolde or her ward Ginny or her new sister-in-law, Lila was the one who knew Violet nearly as well as Victor. "Why are you suspicious?" Violet asked.

"I think she was too ready with your name. And the details of your life. Coincidence? I don't think so. Head's up, darling. Something's afoot."

Violet's brows lifted and she nodded. She supposed if she had been thinking less about her stepmother, Jack, Jack's career, and her brother leaving in the next week, she might have realized what Lila had pointed out.

"You're a good sidekick, love."

"I'm not a sidekick," Lila said. "I'm the love interest of a lazy hero."

Violet snorted so hard on her laughter she fell into a coughing fit and had to dab her tears away before her makeup was destroyed. "That you are, my love."

CHAPTER 3

*R*ita Russell's house was directly next door to Violet's family town home. The earl's family had owned the London monstrosity since time immemorial. It was one of those ancient houses that had been handed down through the generations and that only the richest of the rich and the most established families owned. The house next door, the one matching the address on Rita Russell's card, was no less monstrous.

Lila and Violet looked at the house, at each other, and then their heads tilted as one. Violet narrowed her eyes. "Something's afoot."

"I've already said that."

"That was delayed agreement."

"Didn't this house used to belong to some rich baron?" Lila asked. "You didn't recognize the address?"

"I didn't read it," Violet admitted. "I simply gave the card to the cabbie. The baron lost all of his money in a gambling hell over the course of a year. They had to sell and mortgage everything."

Lila's brows lifted and then she laughed. "I'm surprised your step-mother didn't offer you up to him."

"She probably would have, but she'd have had to murder his wife."

"Who knew your stepmother had limits?"

14

Violet's laugh was a little evil as she agreed. "Do you think that Miss Russell knows my stepmother?"

"Yes," Lila said almost fiercely.

"My stepmother knows where I shop. She took me often enough when I had to let my father buy my clothes. It was the way she kept her claws in."

"She did."

"What are they planning?" Violet asked Lila, who shrugged. They both glanced between the two mansions.

"Maybe Miss Russell has a handsome brother or cousin." Lila wasn't joking, and the fact that Violet had purchased her wedding dress, reserved the church, and was planning her honeymoon while her stepmother was actively trying to destroy the wedding made her cheekbones and teeth ache.

"I don't know," Violet muttered. "Rita is awfully brown. She knew Africa almost as if by experience. My stepmother would hate that. Despise it. Mock it over tea with whomever would listen to her. And to be able to buy that house? It would have to be new money. Lady Eleanor would despise *new* money."

"Would it have to be new money?"

"Certainly," Violet answered. They were both from rich, established families, but being an earl's daughter gave her a perspective that few could attain. "Old money already owns houses like that one. They've all owned them since the dawn of time."

"It's possible that Miss Russell has her own plans. Your stepmother may be trying to use the tools at hand, and Miss Russell is up to something else. Something beyond what Lady Eleanor is planning."

Violet opened the auto door and stepped out of the vehicle. "I'm not playing games with these women. Should we just leave?"

"We should get the lay of the land," Lila said, rubbing her hands together and grinning evilly.

Violet sighed. "Like soldiers examining enemy terrain."

"We shall have to be our own scouts. Well," Lila's head cocked and she winked, "I suppose I am, yet again, being your minion."

"See," Violet teased, "you're no love interest for a lazy hero. You're a sidekick to a cheeky heroine."

They approached the front door of the mansion together, with Violet reaching out and using the door knocker. A very tall, very black man in a perfectly pressed suit opened the door. He lifted his brows in a snobbery that the earl's butler could never match. Violet liked him immediately. She put on her earl's daughter persona and handed her card to him between two fingers.

His eyes glinted in appreciation though none of his feeling spread to his face, and he slowly stepped back. "Miss Russell is expecting you. This way please."

Violet and Lila followed him through the house. She'd been in the mansion before, but the mural on the ceiling had been expertly refreshed, and she had to keep herself from stopping to stare. It had always been lovely, but restored as it was made it a true work of art. The black and white tiles were shining so that Violet could see her reflection in the black tiles.

They were led through the house and down the hall to a sun-filled conservatory that had a table set up under an orange tree.

"Lady Violet, Mrs. Lancaster," the butler announced. He almost, but didn't quite, click his heels together and then spun smoothly and silently exited.

"He's delightful," Violet announced loudly, so he heard her as he closed the doors. "Well now, Miss Russell."

The blonde woman looked up and grinned. "He is, isn't he? I don't think I've ever seen an expression on his face. I'm so glad you've come."

As she spoke, the door opened again, and a very young, very curvaceous, very beautiful woman came into the conservatory. "Oh, how delightful! You've arrived."

Miss Russell's face froze, then a brittle, society smile appeared as she cleared her throat. In a perfectly appropriate and perfectly furious tone, she introduced them. "Lady Violet, Mrs. Lancaster, may I present Mrs. Russell." She paused for a moment and then added, "My stepmother."

Lila faked a sneeze to hide her reaction and then dabbed her mouth with her handkerchief to hide the evil grin. Violet lifted an imperious brow at the woman—girl really—who had paled.

"So nice to meet you," Violet said.

"I wasn't aware you intended to join us," Miss Russell said to the little blonde, who shot Miss Russell a look that so clearly commanded her to be quiet that Violet had to swallow her gasp. This *stepmother* was at least five years younger than Rita Russell and probably more.

"Who doesn't want to meet an earl's daughter!" the girl gushed. "Such a notorious one at that. I *have* heard so much about you."

Miss Russell shot Violet an unreadable glance and seated them at the little table near the teacart.

"Well," Violet said, taking a seat. Lila sat immediately next to her, and they both pasted polite smiles on their faces. Violet glanced around the conservatory. "What lovely orchids."

Miss Russell's lips thinned as Mrs. Russell tittered. "That wasn't quite the thing to say, was it?" the girl admitted. "I'm so glad that dear Rita is home. She can help me with these things. Do forgive me."

Violet glanced at Miss Russell, whose eye twitched. She pressed a finger to her temple before pouring a cup of tea and asking how the others took theirs.

"I'm just so excited to see if you'll accept the sponsorship," Mrs. Russell said. "I confess I wanted it dreadfully, but I understand that dear Rita offered it to you first. The Piccadilly Ladies Club! What an exciting place to see and be seen. I'm sure I'll join you eventually."

The desperate, pleading look Rita Russell threw Violet's way clarified the woman's purposes. She needed Violet to lie for her. Internally, Vi shrugged, then she lied. "Oh! I wish I had known. I'm afraid I've already accepted and joined."

The woman—girl, certainly—pouted. She out and out pouted, and Violet wanted to smack her. She had married a man well past the age to be her father. It was past time to grow up. The horror of the girl's marriage was enough to turn Violet's stomach, thinking of some of her father's friends. If Violet was following what was happening here, and she was stringing together the sparsest of clues, this girl seemed to be not just married to Rita's father but encroaching on Rita's life.

Rita would have been hard-pressed to find another woman as likely to sympathize as Violet. The idea of Lady Eleanor, Violet's own stepmother, trying to encroach into more than an occasional luncheon or weekend in the country was enough to make Violet shudder. Her attempts to upend Violet and Jack's wedding was likely to give Violet migraines on a daily basis.

"Oh, that does make me sad," Mrs. Russell said, turning her cornflower blue eyes up at Violet and blinking slowly, as if Violet would somehow succumb to the pleading there.

"I am afraid, Melody, that it's time for us to discuss *secret* club business. As much as we'd love to have your company, Lady Violet and Mrs. Lancaster only have a short amount of time to spend. You'll understand better than I, given Lady Violet is in the midst of her wedding preparations and can only spare that short amount of time."

"Oh I do!" the girl said, clapping her hands and leaning forward with a bright smile. "Perhaps I can be of assistance."

Lila choked on a laugh again as Violet struggled to find an appropriate reply. She finally said, "I do appreciate the offer ever so! I'm afraid, however, my own stepmother would be so displeased if I turned to another *experienced* woman for help during this time."

Mrs. Russell's pout returned, and she flounced from the conservatory a moment later.

"What," Lila demanded the second the door shut behind the child-bride, "in the world was that? I feel certain that I have descended into some sort of wonderland."

"As do I," Miss Russell said.

"My dear Miss Russell," Lila said, reaching for her hand, "You have brought me to a rare—very rare—moment of sympathy."

Violet was the one choking laughter as Lila patted Miss Russell's hand.

"Rita, please. My goodness, after that I feel as though you've seen my knickers. Thank you for understanding so quickly, Lady Violet."

"Violet, please," Vi replied. "This is Lila. Every time you say Mrs.

Lancaster, I feel certain my brother's mother-in-law is about to appear. It's enough to send me into endless rounds of glancing over my shoulder and examining my word choice."

Lila laughed. "After that I shall need something sweet."

Rita handed over the plate of biscuits and petit fours. Lila took one and handed it to Violet.

"So you *did* hunt us up when we were shopping?"

Rita blushed. "Yes. I asked your sister where to shop. She said, 'My sister is who you need to ask.' Then she listed several shops. I was looking for you, it's true, but to be perfectly honest, I'd have begged anyone I thought might help, and that boutique does cater to the right clientele for my needs."

Violet sipped her tea, and Rita sighed. "Shall I tell you the whole terrible story?"

"Yes," Lila said. "I do love horrible stories, especially if they're true stories."

Rita laughed. "I'll begin with my mother, so you can understand my horror. She was an adventuress! Daring, beautiful, charming, and my father adored her. They raised me as they traveled the world, with father working wherever we went. She died in India about five years ago. Father returned to England. He never had the same love of travel as Mother."

Violet took a cucumber sandwich, feeling as though a quintessentially British food must be the choice she made for a story of returning to England.

"I," Rita continued, "didn't really want to come home, so I begged my aunt to travel with me. It seemed as though I could keep Mama alive that way. I traveled with my mother's sister, later with a few friends. I went all over India, then to Egypt, eventually Africa."

"We guessed that one." Lila's lazy voice had Violet fighting a grin.

"This time when I came home, I thought I'd get Father to go fishing with me in Scotland, perhaps a ramble in the Lake Country. I wanted to go to South America, but I thought I had better visit Father first."

"Get to the good part," Lila demanded.

"When I got home, I found he had married. He told me he wrote me a letter, only it missed me on my surprise return journey."

"So you had a surprise stepmother. Truly, my condolences." Violet shuddered for Rita.

"And *what* a stepmother," Lila crowed without an ounce of sympathy. The cold, cruel creature was enjoying Rita's pain all too much. "How old is she?"

"She's nineteen."

Violet set her teacup down while Lila laughed evilly.

"Nineteen years old," Rita said slowly, as though it needed to be repeated for herself. She seemed to be still half in shock.

"You are—?" Violet had to know.

"Twenty-seven." Rita set down her teacup and rose. "If that weren't bad enough, she goes to parties with my friends. She insinuated herself in with them while I was gone. And as if it couldn't get any worse, I found that she wears my dresses."

"Your dresses?" Violet demanded. "No!"

"She'd say we're the same size, but we aren't. She's far more bosomy than I. She looks like a two-bit streetwalker in my clothes."

Lila waved off the concern. "She's going to be fat in five years. Or fat as soon as she gives your father a child."

"Oh!" Rita shivered. "Don't say that."

"That is bad," Lila told Violet. "If not for the clothes, you might be able to make an argument that the stepmother wasn't trying to take over Rita's life. The clothes, however—those are alarming."

"I would be furious if someone helped themselves to my clothes," Violet admitted, thinking of her rather excessive wardrobe. Even before she'd inherited so nicely from her great-aunt, Violet had spent most of her money on books and clothes.

"I just...I can't...I can't carry on like this," Rita said, dropping into her seat. "I lied to her. I told her I had offered my sponsorship to the ladies club to someone else. I told her I couldn't possibly go back on it. Not to this woman. An earl's daughter!" Rita said, laughing. "Piccadilly doesn't even have us join like that. I made it all up. She's going to find out, and then she'll tell my father, and then I'll be in the doghouse for wanting to have my own life. My goodness, it's just not right! That's my club, my refuge, and to have that giggling child appear and demand my friends' acceptance?" She shook her head. "Do you know how you qualify for joining? You have to be well-connected and educated, like the both of you, or be outstanding in some way. A woman reporter like Miss Allen or an author like you, Violet. And that doesn't count the rumors of your business acumen and charity work."

"We're both joining this club," Lila said. "You, however, Rita, need to do something else. Why don't you just go to South America?"

"I am enjoying London," Rita confessed. "I decided to approach England like I do other countries and explore. It's so much fun. Also, Father—he's all I have. Look what happened after I left him last time. He ended up married to grasping, pouting child. He seems surprised every time she pops up and asks for something. I think he tells her yes just to make her go away."

"Oh dear," Lila said.

"Your father is a grown man and quite an experienced one," Violet countered. "He might have been manipulated by this woman, but this is your life."

"I'm not ready to leave England yet," Rita insisted earnestly.

"Don't," Violet said. "Don't let her drive you away. But wearing your clothes and insinuating herself into your life? No. Move in with your aunt, with a friend, into a hotel if you must. But distance is a requirement."

"I—" Rita glanced between them. "Something must be done."

"Indeed," Violet agreed, while Lila simply held up her teacup and declared, "Hear, hear!"

CHAPTER 4

"There you are," Jack said and Violet spun. She had just left the ballroom where she'd been having her jiu jitsu lesson. She was sweaty and probably smelled, but she threw herself into his arms and kissed his cheek. She'd had to make a bit of a leap to reach his shoulders since he was so much taller than her, but he caught her without an issue.

His dark hair was ruffled from the wind and his dark eyes were fixed on her face. He was not a very expressive man, but she caught the glint in his eyes and she just had to press another kiss on his jaw. He held her against his chest, and her feet dangled off the floor.

"There *you* are!" She tried to avoid a squeal, but she couldn't quite hold it back. "Are you done with your case already or just back for a day or two?"

Jack pressed a kiss on her forehead and then her lips. "The case wrapped up rather quickly. I fear the murderer disposed of the weapon rather terribly. Once we found it, everything fell together."

Violet linked her arms around him and apologized for her sweatiness. "Are you back for a while?"

"I plan on it. Ham knows I don't want to leave, especially while

Victor and Kate are house shopping. Shall we go with them and see the houses?"

"I would love to," Violet told him, hesitating, "and I love Ham for keeping you home. Only—"

He waited, his eyes warm on her face, and Victor ran up the steps to outside of the ballroom. "Are you just going to stand there holding her off the ground?"

"Don't you have a wife to look after?" Jack asked idly, letting Violet down, though he kept hold of one of her hands.

"I do," Victor said. "I'm keeping my twin, however, so you'll just have to look forward to my pretty face."

Jack held out his other hand and they shook, Victor grinning shamelessly and Jack pretending he wasn't pleased to see Victor.

"You two are precious," Violet told them both, letting go of Jack's hand. "I believe I shall go refresh myself and meet you downstairs. You are staying?"

"I need to see to a few things at the yard," Jack said. "What if I return this evening for dinner? I wanted to let you know I was back. The Savoy?"

"Yes," Violet said, "that does sound lovely."

"We'll come," Victor said. "Who doesn't love the Savoy?"

"No," Jack replied flatly. "We'll meet you later at a club. You choose which one."

Victor's grin remained steady as he lifted his brow, but Jack didn't cave. Victor finally clapped Jack on the shoulder. "You win, but you're buying the cocktails."

Jack didn't object and Violet hurried down the stairs and into her bedroom. She had an appointment with her man of business before luncheon and plans to join Lila and Denny afterward for lunch.

She dressed in a navy blue dress with a pleated skirt and a white blouse, adding a grey and white jumper over her blouse. She completed the ensemble with her grey wool jacket and black cloche. She wore sturdy shoes for London's winter. It was wet and cold outside with the type of chill that blew right through one's bones.

Violet dressed rather quickly and hurried from the house, taking a black cab to her appointment. She found Rita Russell in the waiting room. Violet paused, examining the woman with her bright blonde hair and brilliant blue eyes. "Are you sure that you haven't decided to take over my life? Your stepmother might have you rather on her side, but—"

"No, no," Rita said with a sniff. "I have to move the money I inherited from my mother. I thought if there was any man who wouldn't condescend to me and who was also excellent at his business, it would be Lady Violet Carlyle's man."

Violet made a slight nod.

Rita spoke as Violet reached the door to the office. "I feel as though I have crossed a boundary. Again. I—I would like to actually be friends. I wonder if I can invite you to dinner?"

Violet considered. She was feeling a bit hunted, but she also agreed with Rita's reasoning. Finding a man of business who didn't try to control an independent woman and who was also trustworthy could be a difficult endeavor. Simply finding another independent woman and discovering her man of business certainly cut the search down.

"Possibly," Violet finally answered. She went into the office and closed the door before speaking.

"Have you met her yet? Miss Russell?"

Mr. Fredericks, her man of business, shook his head. "Do you want me to refuse her business?"

Violet tilted her head. "Would you do that?"

"You're not just my most profitable client, Lady Violet. You're my favorite."

Violet laughed. "I trust you to keep my business private."

"Of course," he said, handing her a cup of Turkish coffee and a scone.

She sipped the coffee. "That is delightful. I would never interfere with your business beyond expecting my own privacy."

Mr. Fredericks nodded, and they finished their business quickly. Violet's eyes widened slightly at the profits, and she asked about finding a house near Lila and Denny for Victor, but on a whim, she told him to look for one for her and Jack as well.

Rita had left by the time Violet exited the office.

"She didn't have an appointment," Mr. Fredericks said as he escorted her out, "so she had her initial meeting with Jones."

Violet let the matter drop. She returned home to her brother and found that he'd dressed for the evening as well. "We have reservations." Victor grinned at his wife and kissed her cheek. "Kate does enjoy the scallop and shrimp bouillabaisse. One can't ignore the needs of an expectant mother."

Violet smacked her brother's arm before running up the steps to her bedroom. She washed quickly and then took out her newest dress. She had purchased it in her first, aborted attempts to buy more exotic lingerie. Instead, she had walked away from those for the loveliest blue dress that gathered just under her chest. She found the blue broach from her mother and pinned it to the dress to accent the gathering, then smoothed the hem, straightening the fringe that ended near her knees. She chose to skip all other jewelry except black pearl earbobs to allow the broach to shine.

Violet added the matching blue headpiece, her new blue shoes with diamond buckles, and then quickly did her makeup. She was running late for her dinner with Jack, but she was delighted to spend the evening together after the last few weeks separated. She had told him he needed to follow the gossip in his investigations more, but he'd just laughed and said the only reason she'd discovered the guilty was because they would gossip with her. He'd ended it with, "the poor, unsuspecting fools."

Violet played with her engagement ring as she glanced through her makeup. Jack did enjoy the darker brick red lipsticks that she sometimes wore. He'd kissed them off of her often enough. Given the glint in Victor's eye, she suspected her twin would do what he could to prevent Jack from doing just that this evening.

WHEN JACK SAW Victor and Kate, his eyes flashed with humor. He took in Kate's exasperated glance at Victor and then held out his hand for Violet.

"Hullo darling," Violet told him.

"I see your brother is up to his usual," Jack replied.

"He does seem to have an inexplicably sudden reservation this evening."

"We, however, have a private table."

"A travesty," Victor cut in. "I'm sure that it can be corrected."

"Mmm." Kate rubbed her belly and winked at Violet. "Victor, I am feeling unwell." Alarm crossed his face and Kate leaned back into her seat. "This monster you've given me is kicking my lungs." She sounded a little breathy, and Victor lifted her into his arms and turned on Jack.

"This round to you, my friend."

"What did you offer her?" Violet asked Jack after Victor carried Kate away.

"I just asked." Jack lifted Violet's fingers to his mouth and pressed a kiss on each of them. "We're allies, she and I."

Violet's grin escaped and she wrapped her arms around his waist. "Will April ever come?"

"I would reply, sooner or later—" Jack paused to press another kiss on her forehead. "But it does feel like later, doesn't it?"

Violet leaned back. "Are we staying? I would be all right with staying. Enjoy the evening, the wireless, a little dancing, cocktails at home."

Jack pressed another kiss to her forehead and one to her cheek and then leaned down. "Victor would never let me have you to myself, my dear."

She grinned at that and her escaping giggle had him pressing his fingers over her mouth.

"Are you choosing his side?"

"Never." Violet kissed the fingers against her mouth. "I chose you."

"He's your twin."

"Which you knew when you asked me to marry you."

"He's not going anywhere. He's going to demand you choose him endlessly."

"I'll switch sides endlessly," Violet told him honestly, "to keep you both on your toes."

Jack grinned at her then, one of those rare full grins that she loved so much, and she felt as though she'd won a prize to sneak one from him when he held them so close.

"I suppose I can accept that," he told her, "as I knew what I was getting into with you, Lady Violet Carlyle."

"Trouble," she told him.

"Trouble," he agreed.

"Fun?" she suggested.

"Fun."

CHAPTER 5

The art deco mirrors at the Savoy glittered with light, making it all the glitzier in the foyer. A band from America was playing on the stage, and the music had Violet shimmying near Jack. He stoically glanced about, taking it all in. As usual, his penetrating gaze flicked from place to place without ever seeming to settle. Violet, however, had little doubt that he'd be able to recall details despite the dimmed lights and clouds of smoke.

Jack tugged Violet, and she glanced up merrily. She'd completely missed the tuxedoed gentlemen who'd approached to show them to their table.

"I asked for a quiet, more private corner. I hope that's all right with you, darling."

"Of course it is," Violet said. "How else will you tell me all about your investigation?"

Jack's quelling look did nothing to stop Violet's curiosity, but her plans were ruined by, "Oh! Oh! Lady Violet. Lady Violet it *is* you."

Both Vi and Jack turned, and Violet groaned just loud enough to be heard by Jack.

"Darling," Violet told him evenly, "may I present Mrs. Russell." Violet looked beyond the lush, young blonde and saw quite an older man. He was tall and trim like his daughter, Rita. His hair had gone gray, but his eyes were the same brilliant blue, and he was rather handsome, really. Any sympathy Violet felt for the girl faded immediately. The man was looking at his young wife as though he could hardly believe she belonged to him—and not in a shocked, delighted way, but the way of a person who realized their diamonds were, in fact, paste.

"Hello," Jack said, holding out his hand to the gentlemen. "Jack Wakefield."

"Frederick Russell, so nice to meet you. My wife," he glanced down at the blonde, "was just telling me about meeting you."

Jack glanced down at Violet curiously, but she could hardly explain while they were looking on. What a strange story to tell as well. "Ah," Jack said, "this is our table. It was a pleasure."

"Perhaps we can put our tables together." Mrs. Russell fluttered her lashes up at her husband.

Jack had become stone under Violet's hand, and Violet cut in. "That does sound delightful. I do, however, intend to keep Jack to myself this evening. I fear I can be quite greedy when it comes to a dinner with Jack after he's been out of town." Violet applied that arrogant air she preferred never to use and smiled brightly as she vaguely promised, "I'm sure we'll see each other soon. Rita is a rather dear friend."

Violet turned her face to Jack, shot him a look, and he nodded at the other two, and they escaped.

"What," Jack demanded as he seated her, "was that?" He ordered them drinks as they relaxed.

Violet nibbled her bottom lip, holding back a laugh. She leaned forward and said dramatically, "It all starts with Miss Emily Allen."

Jack's gaze zeroed in on her so completely, she felt certain she could feel the movement of his eyes over her face. "What does Emily have to do with it?"

Violet lifted a brow, crossed her arms over her chest, and shot him a nasty look.

"Miss Allen."

Violet's laugh escaped. "I was only—"

"Yes, yes." Jack waved his hand.

"So Em," Violet told him. "She is a member of this Piccadilly Ladies Club where a Miss Rita Russell is also a member. Apparently, Miss Russell asked her for the name of a rather—how shall we describe me?"

"A pearl of great price?" Jack teased.

"Victor says I have overused that one," Violet told him. "An inexplicably notorious yet well-connected female."

"One perhaps who has solved a murder or two to the consternation of a certain escaped fiancé."

"Escaped?" Violet laughed. "As though a lion from the zoo."

"Better than that," Jack declared, taking a drink of his old-fashioned. "Far better than that. As though I could fly."

"Very smooth," Violet told him, raising her glass.

Jack's expression was smooth innocence. Their dinner arrived, and Violet's expression widened as she looked beyond Jack. "By Jove! Jack! Is that the same dress that Mrs. Russell is wearing?"

Jack glanced behind him, saw Rita Russell—having no idea who she was—and nodded. "The same dress Mrs. Russell is wearing? Yes, I believe so. She is, however, made for that gown. It looks like it would on you. Isolde is a bit, ah—more abundant, like Mrs. Russell. She'd never wear that gown."

"Jack," Violet declared, "are you a follower of women's fashion?"

"I have eyes," Jack told her with the tiniest of smirks.

"Do you?"

"I might admire the feminine form."

"Might you?" She tried pressing her lips to hide the smile, but it didn't work. "Jack," Violet told him, "that beautiful, bronzed blonde is Rita Russell. Her stepmother, the child bride, bought the same dress."

"I don't know what that means," Jack lied, grinning at her.

"Yes, you do," Violet countered. "You just want me to explain, knowing it sounds ridiculous for being quite so petty. You're a cheeky lad."

Jack and Violet ate in companionable silence. When they were nearly finished, Violet spoke. "Lila and Denny will be at the club."

"Do you think Kate has confessed?"

"I think Victor realized the moment that Kate said she was ill. Victor has become domestic."

"You know that now?" Jack asked. "I saw that whole thing too. He lifted her up and carried her out of the room."

"He did," Violet agreed.

"So how do you know anything else?"

"He *didn't* check her forehead, frantically send for a doctor, or glance about helplessly and beg for assistance. He lifted her up—quite romantically, I might add."

"And carried her to the bedroom. An act I understand."

"By Jove, Mr. Wakefield. What an unaccountable conversation for the dinner table."

They finished their dinner, but the look Jack gave Violet turned her quite red. They left soon after, and as they got into the auto Jack had arranged, Violet glanced back and saw that Mrs. Russell was leaving along with Rita and her date. Mr. Russell loaded them into an auto and left on foot.

"Look, Jack," Violet said, poking him in the side. "That child bride has wriggled her way into Rita's date. Can you imagine?"

Jack glanced back. "I can. She tried the same with us, love."

When Jack handed Violet out of the black cab, she choked. "Jack!"

He glanced around, alert, and then cursed. "Why are they following us?"

Violet shook her head helplessly, but she feared she knew. If Rita's life had filled Melody Russell with envy, what would an earl's daughter's do to the woman? Vi glanced at Jack and then back at the other auto. She sighed and confessed, "She's in love, my love. With my title."

"You're taken. She'll have to move along."

"I fear I shall have to be rude," Violet told him.

"Better you than me, my love."

She laughed. "One evening. We'll dance and have drinks. I don't —I don't want to become my stepmother. I could put on my air and

I could look down my nose at her and lift my brow and say something snide, but I would destroy her, and I don't want to be that person."

"Yet another reason I adore you, Vi. We'll dance and have drinks. Perhaps if we slide in, we can avoid them for a while."

Violet and Jack ran up the steps. They both heard the faint call of "Oh, Lady Violet!" but neither stopped.

Jack and Violet handed their coats over quickly and rushed into the club. Rather than going for a cocktail, they almost jumped into the dancing. The band was amazing, and the singer had a voice that made Violet jealous.

"Shall we risk stopping?" Violet panted after several songs. "I could do with a cocktail."

Jack touched his finger to her chin, tipped her head up, and kissed her forehead. They worked their way through the crowd. There was a line at the bar, but Jack simply used his bulk to flag a waiter to them, handed over a large bill, and asked for cocktails.

"There's a unique one tonight, sir," the man said with glee-filled eyes.

Jack glanced at the crowd, down at Vi, and said, "We'll take two Bee's Knees and two of the unique one. What is it?"

"It's a rhubarb and fennel cocktail. The barman was exultant about some hothouse stuff that came in. There's a table over near the stage opening up," he added.

Jack nodded and they made their way to the table where the waiter cleared it quickly. "I'll be back in half a mo'."

"Jack," Violet said as she glanced around. "We have room at our table, and we've been caught."

Jack took her hand, playing with her fingers as he waved the waiter over. "Bring some of them as well."

The waiter nodded, caught the sight of the two blondes and two men with close cut beards. "I actually had an order from them a moment before you."

"Never mind then," Violet said, "You're a good man."

Jack lit a cigarette as the foursome joined them.

"What wonderful luck!" Mrs. Russell said. "I thought we saw you come in here."

The glance from Rita standing behind the child bride and the smirk from the man who had a hand on Rita's waist proclaimed that a lie.

"How fortunate," Violet said, "that we've run into each other before we dance a little more. I told Jack I needed two drinks, another half hour of dancing, and my bed."

Rita accepted the cocktail from the waiter and raised the glass to Vi with twitching lips. They were all handed pretty pink drinks with curls of rhubarb. Violet took her Bee's Knees first and sipped and then took up the rhubarb one.

"Oh," Mrs. Russell pouted, "I didn't get one with a curl of rhubarb."

Violet handed her second drink over. "Have mine, dear."

"Do you want mine?" Mrs. Russell asked, smiling prettily.

"I'll just have a sip of Jack's," Violet told the woman.

Mrs. Russell's red lipstick was smeared, and Violet noted the corresponding orange-red on the collar of the second man. He didn't seem to care in the least that she was married or that her stepdaughter was watching in disgust as he leaned too close and kept his eyes cast in a rather lewd direction.

The conversation was stilted over the sound of the music, but Mrs. Russell at least was bright with her fluttering lashes and smiles. Violet tried not be drawn in by her. They listened to several songs, finishing their drinks and ordering more. Again, Mrs. Russell was served a drink without a rhubarb curl. Her gaze narrowed on the waiter and she scolded him ferociously, but Jack over-tipped to compensate.

Violet sipped Jack's rhubarb and fennel cocktail and scrunched her nose. "Oh! That is sour!" She twisted her mouth and returned to her cocktail. She laid her head against Jack's shoulder for just a moment and caught Rita's gaze on them. Rita shook her head slightly, and Violet lifted her head to find the sharp, avaricious gaze of Mrs. Russell.

"Ladies," Violet informed Jack. "I am sorry."

He squeezed her fingers. "I can abide it, darling. Only return soon."

When Violet rose, Rita rose as well. They were followed a moment later by Mrs. Russell, and Jack shot Violet a commiserating look.

In the ladies, Violet dabbed the back of her neck with a wet cloth. Her lipstick had smeared just a little, though it was from drinking and talking and dancing.

"How fun that we found you," Mrs. Russell cooed. She shimmied into the mirror, adjusting her breasts, which were barely held in by the dress designed for a straight, slim figure. "I know your figure is the fashion, dear Violet."

"It's Lady Violet," Rita snapped, reapplying her lipstick.

"Oh yes, of course, I just thought we were all friends here when I saw how cozy Violet was with Jack. Does your stepmother know things have progressed? I understand from Rita's friends that there are ways to prevent unwanted consequences." Mrs. Russell smiled prettily and leaned in to reapply her lipstick, but her hand was shaking.

Violet's gaze narrowed, and she saw through a fury-red gaze. "What is it you mean by that comment?"

"What is it that you think I mean?" Mrs. Russell asked, placing her hand over her heart.

"I think you assume you have some measure of control over me," Violet told her simply, "because you can see that I am comfortable with the man I'm about to marry. You also assume that Lady Eleanor, the earl's *third* wife, has some measure of control of the independently wealthy, well-connected, educated daughter of the earl. Let me be clear. I supported myself before my inheritance, I control and conduct business interests, I write successful books, and I will not be blackmailed or manipulated. I will certainly not be blackmailed or manipulated by an upstart, child-bride of a man with a fortune of new money. No offense intended, Rita. I suspect I'll rather like you."

"None taken," Rita said smoothly.

"What?" Mrs. Russell squealed, and she stumbled back. "You are my stepdaughter. Do you think that your father will allow…" She took a deep breath in, shuddered, and gasped again. "Allow…allow you to speak to me like that?"

"My father and I are well aware of where I stand." Rita leaned back, crossing her arms over her chest. "We had a long talk about it today, and he's well aware that I am done putting up with your nonsense. You'll find I've moved into The Hotel Saffron when you return home. Father has accepted that you are his burden to bear."

"I—" Mrs. Russell stumbled back again, grasping onto the counter behind her. "I...I..." Her horrified gaze darted between the two women, and then she slid down onto the floor.

"What is this? Some...some...game?" Rita demanded.

Violet touched Mrs. Russell's cheek. Her eyes rolled towards Violet and then rolled back.

The door to the ladies room opened and a cigarette girl stepped in. Violet glanced at her. "You! Go get the very large man at the table near the stage. He's quite broad, with dark hair, dark eyes, and he answers to Jack. Tell him Violet needs a doctor immediately."

The girl started in surprise. Violet snapped. "Now! Run!"

Rita dropped onto her knees next to Violet. "What is wrong?"

"She can't talk, Rita," Violet told her. "She's trembling. She fell. Something is very wrong."

CHAPTER 6

*J*ack pushed through the ladies room door and took in the sight of Violet holding Mrs. Russell.

"Did someone send for a doctor?" Violet demanded.

Jack nodded, lifting Mrs. Russell and laying her on the sofa in the corner of the ladies room. "What happened?" he asked. His voice and jaw were both tight, and Violet felt that familiar anxiety rising in her stomach. This was bad. It was *really* bad, and she did *not* need to add to her nightmares. She closed her eyes and ordered herself to focus

"We were arguing," Violet told him, taking Mrs. Russell's hand. The girl's breathing was jerky and she didn't seem to be capable of speech, but she moaned often enough to show she was in pain. "She —" Violet thought back. "She was trembling. She'd just said something awful, but she had trouble putting on her lipstick. Don't you think that's when she started to act odd, Rita?"

Rita's gaze was wide and horrified, and she stumbled over her words. "I...I really don't know. She's too young to fall ill. Isn't she?" Those big blue eyes darted about the ladies room.

"Yes," Jack snapped. Several waiters came into the ladies, and they carried Mrs. Russell to the ambulance. "Violet, you need to come tell the doctor what you saw."

She nodded and hurried after him. The coat girl brought Violet and Jack their coats while Mrs. Russell was loaded into the ambulance. Violet and Jack followed in a black cab that was held waiting for them. In the auto, Violet faced Jack.

"Maybe she's having a reaction to something she ate."

"I think we need to talk to Mr. Russell." Jack's voice was low and dark, and Violet shivered. He wrapped his arm around her, but she wasn't cold. It *was* cold, but the issue was more that his voice told her he was concerned.

"We aren't sick," Violet told him, thinking of the fact that they'd had all the same drinks and eaten at the same restaurant. "It can't be something like bad mushrooms, right? Maybe she's just overheated." She sounded a little frantic, but she'd barely shaken the last round of nightmares.

Jack pressed a kiss to the top of her head. "Darling Vi, don't worry. I'm sure it's just like you said."

She would have shot him a look that said he was a fool for trying to manipulate her into believing such an outright lie, but she knew he was trying to comfort her. She wound their fingers together and when the car stopped, she saw Mrs. Russell be rushed from the ambulance. She was vomiting. Violet pressed her face into Jack's shoulder.

Her conscience was battling with her desire to avoid further nightmares. She *did* feel a bit bad about the woman. Violet did not like Mrs. Russell, but Vi also wouldn't wish a terrible illness on anyone.

Jack hurried her up the stairs, their fingers tangled together, and his bulk made a path through the busyness of the hospital. The fellows carrying Mrs. Russell were murmuring to each other, and Violet both wanted to know what they were saying and wanted to know what they were not saying.

Jack called over a local police constable who had escorted in a dazed man, and he recapped what had happened to the woman. "We need to know if her husband is also ill," Jack told the constable. "You'll have to hunt up his address, if you can. The stepdaughter is on her way here, so you can get the address from her."

Violet interrupted with the address and directions, and the

constable nodded. As he left the hospital a man appeared with a white coat and a stethoscope on his neck. His eyes were tight and his face was concerned. "You were with the woman who just came in?"

Jack answered while Violet watched a woman bring in a child with a broken arm. The boy was wailing, and it seemed all she could hear was the crying—nothing else. Through it all, it felt like someone was speaking to her, but she couldn't hear anything else.

"Vi," Jack near shouted, tipping her face towards his and cupping her cheeks. "Are you all right?"

"The boy," Violet said, shaking her head, and the haze of the moment snapped away as quickly as it had come. "I'm sorry. What do you need from me?"

The doctor's concern had increased, and he insisted they step into an examination area. He asked her what they'd eaten, what they'd drank. While he asked her questions, he listened to her heart and lungs, tested her reflexes, and looked into her eyes.

"Is she all right?" Jack demanded. The growl in his voice had her looking up in concern.

"I think she's in shock. Take her home, keep her warm, keep a close eye on her. Her breathing, her temperature, all of it. You are her husband?"

"Her fiancé," Jack answered.

The doctor nodded. "Just to be sure, don't leave her alone. Someone needs to make sure her breathing doesn't alter, just in case."

"What do you think is happening with Mrs. Russell?"

"I'm afraid that might be a matter for the yard," the doctor replied.

"I'm Detective Inspector Jack Wakefield," Jack said, holding out his card.

"Her symptoms are that of poisoning," the doctor said. "Dr. Hannity is working on her. Hopefully, we can help her."

"What do you think it could be?" Jack asked again.

"I don't know, not yet. I'll contact you. Take your fiancé home."

"She's fine, though, yes?"

"It's only shock," the doctor said.

If he'd introduced himself, Violet hadn't noticed.

She took a deep breath. "I'm all right, darling. Just tired and—abysmally horrified."

Jack took Violet home, and she wanted nothing more than to strip off of her evening gown, put on a pair of pajamas, and curl up in her bed, but Jack's penetrating hawk gaze followed her every move.

"I'm all right. I just—I feel like any time anything bad happens around us, it'll feed those nightmares, and then I panic, as though all my progress of stopping them will be lost, and I'll be back to not enough sleep and more blues, and I'm trying so hard to be happy."

Jack cupped her face again, placing a kiss on her forehead. "Nightmares are reasonable things to have after witnessing something awful. I've had them and do have them."

"What do you dream about?"

Jack had taken her hand and was leading her up the stairs to her bedroom. "I've lost my mother, so many close friends during the war, my last cousin in the large influenza outbreak after the war, one of my oldest friends in an auto accident just before I met you. Now, though, when I dream terrible things, Vi—it's you. I dream about losing you."

Her eyes burned at his answer, at the emotion that he had let show in his voice, let alone the realization of what she meant to him. She pulled him to a stop and hugged him tightly.

"This is what we're going to do," he told her in a low voice, since Victor's room was just down from Violet's. "Change into your sleep clothes, and I'll stay with you, just to be sure."

Violet paused and then offered, "I could get Beatrice."

"I won't sleep regardless, Vi—not with you at risk. Like I said, we all have our nightmares. I need my eyes on you and the surety that Beatrice didn't slip into sleep by mistake."

Violet didn't argue. She glanced at her brother's door before hurrying into her bedroom. Her dog Rouge jumped from the end of her bed, stretched dramatically, and trotted over. Violet leaned down and scratched the dog's ears and chin.

Beatrice had laid out a pair of brick red pajamas and one of Violet's kimonos. Vi took them both and went into the bath to quickly wash her face, brush her teeth, and change her clothing. Rouge had followed Violet in, and the dog watched her every move. She took off her earbobs and placed them carefully in a bowl to the side of the sink and then pressed cream into her skin.

She wasn't quite sure what to think of Jack watching her while she slept. She knew if there was the merest chance that she could be affected as Mrs. Russell was that Jack would never leave her side. Even still, she wasn't mentally prepared for the shift between them.

The day was quickly coming that they would sleep together nightly, yet somehow it felt odd to have him in her room early. Even though she wanted nothing more than the comfort of his arms.

When she exited the bathroom, she found Victor and Jack whispering in the hallway. Rouge followed Vi and stopped when she stopped. The little dog's head tilted as she examined the two men, and then she trotted over and placed a solitary paw on Jack's foot.

"Are you all right, Vi?" Victor asked immediately. He crossed to her and took her face, tilting her eyes towards the light as though he might notice an illness in them.

"I'm fine." She hugged him tight and pulled away. "Spooked, yes. But darling Victor, all is well. Do not be concerned."

Victor's gaze narrowed on her, and she watched him examine her thoroughly. He even took her pulse and watched her breathe before he finally dropped her wrist. "She seems all right," Victor told Jack.

"The doctor said the way she acted was probably shock, not whatever was wrong with Mrs. Russell."

"This isn't her first body or accident or illness," Victor said, wrapping his arm around Violet's shoulders. "Why is she in shock?"

"I think that's the problem," Jack answered. "No one should see the terrible things we do to each other as members of the human race. Let alone Violet. She's too empathetic."

Victor didn't argue, and Violet felt as though they were stripping her bare.

"I'll stay with her," Victor told Jack.

"You are about the only person I would entrust with her," Jack said, "but I'm staying." The statement was flat and there was no room for argument.

Victor, of course, immediately began to argue.

"Go, Victor," Violet snapped. "It'll be fine."

"Vi," Victor started, and she shot him such a furious look that he flinched and left, but he kept the door open.

Jack snorted at the sight of the open door and turned to Violet. There was an unlit fire in the fireplace, so he lit it before taking a seat.

"No," Violet told him, as he started to arrange the two seats near the fire into a sort of upright bed.

"I can see you from here."

"You can see me from beside me."

"Your father and brother might slaughter me."

"The last I heard," Violet told him with a smile, "we are getting married in three months. I'm not saying that we need to—ah—" She blushed brilliantly and then muttered, "I just think it might be all right if I—if we—"

Jack stood, lifted Violet into his arms and carried her to the bed. The covers had been pulled back and he set her down. He grinned at her for a moment before leaning down and kissing her forehead. Then he took her thick quilt and pulled it up to her chin.

"Jack?" she asked, but he rounded the bed and joined her, sitting upright against her headboard on top of the blankets.

She turned onto her side, propped her head on her hand, and shook her head at him.

"Yes?"

She wasn't quite sure how to say it. She was both very ready for and very nervous about their wedding night, and she knew he'd committed to himself to wait until after their wedding. She wasn't quite sure why, but she thought it might be that pedestal he'd put her on. She was all right with his pedestal, since he was on one of her own making.

"I want you to hold me," she told him honestly, biting her lip. Her gaze was to the side, so she didn't see him stand, take off his tie and jacket and then lay on her bed once again. A few moments later, he lay down next to her and she snuggled closer, placing her head on his chest below his shoulder where she could hear his heartbeat.

41

After a long moment, he wrapped his arm around her. She took a deep breath in and realized that not so long from now this might be how she slept every night. She trembled.

"Do you want children right away?" she asked.

"Do you?"

"I don't know," Violet admitted. "I think I might once we meet Violet Junior. What do *you* want?"

Jack kissed the top of her head and tangled their fingers together. "Just you."

Before Violet could reply, Rouge leapt onto the bed and wormed her way between Violet and Jack, tail wagging. "Looks like Rouge objects."

Jack kissed the top of her head. Their murmured conversation eventually ended when Violet succumbed to exhaustion. Before she fell asleep, she got used to the feel of Jack checking her pulse and pressing to just below her collarbones to check her rate of breathing. She had little doubt as sleep pulled her under that Jack would spend what remained of the night continuing to check her breathing and pulse until he was utterly certain she was well.

CHAPTER 7

"Your man is here," Victor told Jack, waking Violet, who gasped. She glanced around blankly. She could only be certain of the fact that she had been sleeping like a baby. Her body still felt heavy, and her brain wanted to curl into Jack's side and sink back into sleep. Jack, she saw, was reading a book next to her. It took her a moment to realize her wrist was in his hand, and he'd been monitoring her pulse the whole night through.

At some point, he'd reached over and taken one of the books, a favorite Edgar Rice Burroughs story, on the table next to her bed and turned on the lamp to read by, but she had entirely slept through it. She had thought that she would certainly have nightmares. Especially with the look of sort of horrified agony in the too-silent Mrs. Russell's gaze the previous day. Violet could only imagine how terrible it must be to be in pain and be unable to speak.

Vi shook off the memory. Victor was standing at the end of the bed with something of a smirk, but his gaze was worried as he asked Jack, "Is she all right?"

"Her pulse and breathing were fine all night. No signs of nausea or confusion. Except for right now." His lips twitched as Violet blinked rapidly, rubbing at her eyes. She felt as though the chains of sleep were still tugging at her.

Victor huffed out in relief. "Your man brought you a suit, Hamilton Barnes, and the doctor from the previous evening. They would very much like to speak with you. I thought you might like to use my razor and what not, so I had Hargreaves set them up in the breakfast room. They'll be bringing in strong coffee and bacon in a few minutes."

"Did they say why they were here so early?" Jack asked, as he rose from the bed. "It can't be good."

Violet bit her bottom lip at the thought. She'd rather go back to fighting with her stepmother instead of facing whatever had brought Hamilton to *Victor's* door so early.

She slid out of the bed and hurried to the bath. She would dress and meet them downstairs as well to see what was going on. When she finished brushing her teeth and washing her face, she exited the bath to discover Jack and Victor were both gone. At some point Beatrice must have gathered the dog. The fire had been tended and Violet saw that the few things she'd left out had been put away.

Violet glanced through her armoire at the dresses that were pressed and prepared and chose a navy blue day dress that flattered her slim figure but wasn't too flashy. It was a relief to concentrate on a task as mundane— but to her exciting—as choosing a dress for the day. It helped to stabilize her.

Violet had little doubt that her brother had appeared randomly over the course of the night. He looked almost as tired as Jack. She would have done the same if it were Victor who was at risk and Kate watching him. She would have fretted over Jack if it were him who had an *episode* with the doctor looking on. She didn't blame either Jack or Victor for hovering.

She dressed quickly once again. This time, she left her freckles out to shine rather than powdering them as she usually did, knowing that Jack liked them. One of the times she'd awoken from sleep the previous evening, she'd felt him tracing them with his index finger. She'd slipped back into sleep to the tender touch.

She drew on her brows, darkened her lashes, and put a touch of pink balm on her lips, then hurried down the stairs.

When she stepped into the breakfast room, the gentlemen rose. She smiled around at them. "Good morning. Doctor, Ham, Jack."

Victor and Kate weren't in the room. Violet made herself a plate of food, a cup of coffee, and joined Jack at the table. He smiled at her, and she grinned at the sight of his already empty plate. She had little doubt he was on—at the least—his second cup of coffee. They were, both of them, overly fond of Turkish coffee. When you added in the sleepless night for Jack, Violet felt they were both excused from overindulging that morning.

Violet lifted her brows, silently asking him to explain why the gentlemen were here. "There's a reason to believe that Mrs. Russell has been poisoned."

"How?" she asked, trying to control her reaction. An accident—even a terrible one—wouldn't give her nightmares. She wanted to look forward to the arrival of Victor's baby without feeling like the poor child was doomed before she even came into the world. "Was it intentional?"

"We're still determining the details," Jack told her. "I'll be going back to the club this evening before they open to speak with the staff, and I'd like to talk to Miss Russell. Hamilton sent someone round to the house, but she isn't there."

"She moved into a hotel," Violet said, hoping that Rita wasn't the poisoner. "I'm not sure she would be there either way. Perhaps she's at the hospital with her father?"

"Mrs. Russell's sister is with her. Mr. Russell left. He doesn't seem to be anywhere."

"Was he also affected?"

Jack shook his head, and the doctor explained. "We spoke with him the previous evening. They had very little overlap. It seems that he chose the seafood, and she had something much simpler."

Violet could imagine how that must have gone. To be honest, Violet imagined that the spoiled, childlike Mrs. Russell probably refused the exotic flavors offered by the Savoy and complained that the food there was unpalatable. Had she eaten bread and whined about Violet and Jack refusing to share a table with them?

"What are you going to do?" Violet asked them. "Is this a case?"

"That remains to be seen, Vi," Hamilton said. "I suppose if it is, Jack will be the natural investigator."

Violet nodded and then suggested, "I might be able to find Miss Russell."

Hamilton's and Jack's gazes met and both of them tried and failed to hold back a wince. "Perhaps," Violet added, "Jack would want to come with me as I did?"

Hamilton huffed. "We only want you to be safe, Vi."

"I can avoid trying to find her," Violet offered. "To be clear, however, I'd rather help your hunt of a new friend than fight with my stepmother about the wedding."

Hamilton hadn't met Lady Eleanor yet, but Violet was already worried about preparing him for the condescending rudeness he'd experience when he did.

"I'd like you to check Violet over again," Jack told the doctor. "If she's recovered, I'll keep her with me."

"She needs quiet and peace, not work," the doctor told Jack, as if Violet weren't sitting right there.

"She needs to feel safe," Jack replied. "We are—all of us—aware that she's having a version of shellshock. She's seen too many bodies and encountered too many murderers and been attacked too many times."

"She has hardly been to war," the doctor scoffed. "It's only a woman's nerves."

"You don't get to judge what she's experienced," Jack snapped coldly. "You have none of the details, and they are none of your business."

"I'd hardly say that," the doctor with a snide tone. "I *am* a doctor."

"Then why don't you make sure she doesn't have whatever Mrs. Russell has. Leave the rest of her care to the doctor who knows her and those who are aware of what we've been through."

The doctor flushed and his eyes narrowed on Jack with an arrogance that proclaimed Jack a big, dumb man needing to be put in his place. "'We' now? I didn't see you sent into a round of shock by a child crying."

Violet blushed furiously. She both wanted to hide behind Jack and box the doctor's ears. However, Violet was not one to hide. And she did know how to box ears, at least verbally.

"I'll have Victor call our own doctor, Jack. This man is clearly better suited to proclaiming his skills rather than practicing them. "

"I can certainly look you over." The doctor sniffed. "Come now."

"Get out," Violet replied, smiling sweetly with her teeth bare. "Don't come back."

"Don't be an idiot."

Jack began to reply, his expression harsh, but Violet placed a hand on his shoulder. "I believe I asked you to leave my house." Her tone was even and cool despite the burning on her cheeks. "Certainly an educated man such as the doctor you claim to be can understand the King's English."

The doctor rose, striding angrily towards the door and muttering about hysterical women as he did.

"Thank you, Jack," Violet told him, rising to refill her own coffee and taking his cup as well. "What an unpleasant man. Ham, would you like more tea? Or are you drinking coffee?" The simple act helped to calm her, both of her anger and her embarrassment.

He nodded and handed over his cup for more Earl Grey tea. She was well aware that Jack would want the family doctor called, and she wasn't going to make him fight with her over it. Besides, it was very early, and she guessed that Rita Russell had escaped to that Piccadilly Ladies Club if she wasn't at the hotel or her home.

The family doctor arrived rather quickly, as they'd reached him before he left his house for his office. He looked Violet over carefully with Jack, Victor, and Kate hovering.

"It must be nice to be so beloved," the doctor said, as he shined his light in Violet's eyes. "What lovely eyes you have. This dark brown is unmatched except, of course, by that brother of yours." He glanced up.

"Her eyes are clear with her pupils responding normally. No concerns there."

He listened to her heart and checked her reflexes and talked to her about the blues and her nightmares. "I understand the depth of your travails, given the extent of your previous injuries," he confessed later in the parlor. They had tea things around them. "I'm hardly surprised you're having nightmares, Violet. Of course you are. Any person who wasn't called to fight against such evils like your Jack or the police would be having them. Those who are called struggle too. They simply bury it in anger or too much drinking or other activities. Jack's guess of shellshock isn't too far wrong."

"What do I do?" Violet asked.

"There isn't any prescribed course of action. Doctors are trying different things the world over for our soldiers who suffer. Some use drugs, some use physical activity, some use quiet. My thoughts on the matter are hardly agreed upon."

"What are they?" Jack asked.

"I think she should try to be active, try to find a hobby like painting or gardening. Something more than your books, my dear, as those have been work for you, I imagine. You don't have to be good at playing an instrument or painting or gardening to find solace in it. One of my patients does very well with journaling. Another has given up all alcohol and sweets. He eats only vegetables and grains."

Violet glanced at Jack and then back at the doctor. "Well, I don't want to do that."

The doctor laughed. "Some days will be better. Some worse. This isn't hysteria or women's megrims. Your soul is struggling, my dear. You've been part of terrible things. Time, distance, love and the good things of life will help your soul to recover."

"And the rest of us?" Jack asked.

"Give her the space to have bad days and give her reasons to have good ones. Violet, you will be fine. I suspect you'll be sleeping quite a bit better in the next few months." There was something of a wicked grin on his face as he glanced at Jack. He patted her hand as he rose.

"Newlyweds the world over sleep better than most, especially those who have been thoroughly threatened by an earl."

"You know about that?" Violet demanded.

"I treat Tomas St. Marks. I merely inferred."

CHAPTER 8

*R*ita wasn't at the hotel. It was about the most perfect hotel Violet had ever visited. There were gargoyles on the roof, arched windows, and a uniformed bellman who might be the most beautiful man that Violet had seen. She paused in sheer shock and Jack glanced back, followed her gaze, and then shook his head.

"He's lovely. Let's find Rita."

"I need another few minutes," Violet said, noting how the doorman preened a little under her gaze. "Oh, no. I'm done."

"Are you sure?" he asked dryly.

She grinned at Jack. "He's prettier than you, but I just like you."

"Love, you mean," Jack told her.

"That too." She pressed up on her toes and daringly put a kiss on his cheek despite the busy street. "Shall we go hunt down our missing bird?"

Jack tugged her back into motion, and they walked up the half circle of stairs that narrowed into the double doors. The doors were a solid, dark wood that shone with polish. The pretty doorman opened the door before they reached it and bowed slightly as they entered. Violet felt the overwhelming weight of the man's gaze. She wasn't sure if she'd been found wanting or not, but she didn't care.

They approached the man behind the counter in the lobby, and again, Violet felt the silent appraisal. Did her expensive shoes, her fur-trimmed coat, or the diamond on her hand cause the polite nod and smile they received?

"Sir. Madam," the man greeted.

Violet squeezed Jack's arm as she said, "Hello, I am Lady Violet Carlyle. I referred Miss Russell to the hotel. Is she in her room?"

"Good morning, my lady," the man said even more politely. "Miss Russell left very early this morning."

"To the Piccadilly Ladies Club?" Violet asked smoothly, with an air of pure Lady Eleanor arrogance.

"Yes, my lady."

"Wonderful," Violet told him. She glanced at Jack. He slid a hand across the counter, and Violet had little doubt that he'd left a rather substantial tip.

As they left, she asked, "Greasing the hinges of his mouth for later?"

Jack smirked. "Not as effectively as that title of yours."

She grinned evilly and winked. "Shall we be good and go hunt her down? Or shall we stop at that chocolatier across the way and indulge?"

"This isn't an official case, and perhaps chocolate and a friendly ear would help Miss Russell remember what happened."

"I like how you think," Violet told him, enjoying the feel of his bicep under her hand. They hurried across the street and bought too much chocolate. The piece they were offered to sample was enough for Violet to order a large box for Denny and Lila and two for Victor's house, one for Violet, one for Victor and Kate. She arranged for delivery; then they took a box for Rita and a small one to share.

"The ones with blueberry are my favorite," Violet told Jack after one melted in her mouth. "I do love candied blueberries or however they make that creamy stuff in the middle."

Jack's chocolate had been painted with gold leaf and infused with coffee. Violet was sure it had been excellent with the bitter coffee smoothed by the sweet milk chocolate, but she didn't regret her choice.

It wasn't far to the Piccadilly Ladies Club, so they decided to walk. It wasn't raining, but it was chilly. Violet tucked herself into Jack's warmth, having little doubt that he'd suggested walking because of the doctor's comment about being active. She guessed he'd be taking her on rambles in the country, horseback riding, bicycling, and swimming far more often. Perhaps she'd find the jiu jitsu instructor suggesting lessons more often.

She laughed at her vision of the future as they approached the ladies club. It was an unassuming brick building with double doors that were manned. A woman wearing the typical butler uniform opened the door for them to enter, and Violet held out her card.

"We're looking for Miss Rita Russell," Violet said.

The woman butler glanced at Jack, back to Violet, and read the card. "There is a small waiting room that you may take your gentlemen fellow in, but he cannot enter beyond that room."

"How lovely and private," Violet said brightly. "Would you tell Miss Russell it's a matter of some urgency?"

"You may come in if you like, Lady Violet. I was given your name as a prospective member just today."

Vi glanced at Jack and he nodded, so she waved the woman forward and followed after. The halls were empty, but the walls were covered with paintings of famous women. Violet liked it immediately. Joan of Arc, Boudicca, along with the more modern women like Marie Curie—the noble laureate and Emmeline Parkhurst. Violet saw Jane Austen and smiled. *Sense and Sensibility* would forever be Violet's favorite book on sisterhood, and it had all the more meaning now that she and Isolde knew each other so much better than they had as children.

Rita Russell was sitting in a chair in the library, staring into the flames with a glass of bourbon at her side.

"Early to have a drink," Violet told Rita.

"Oh," Rita said. She frowned at Vi. "Violet?"

"You *are* a quick study," Violet told her, and then saw she was wearing the same black evening gown. Her eyes were red and blood-shot with rather cavernous puffiness underneath. "Oh you do look terrible. Are you all right, my dear?"

Rita shook her head helplessly. "I left the hospital and went to the hotel, but—"

"Is it bad?"

"They don't think she'll live," Rita said slowly. "They—it's just a matter of time. She isn't even aware anymore. You know what's the worst of it? I was—I was so sure Father regretted her. But he broke down and wept in my arms. He said she was a ray of sunshine, so happy about the littlest things. Like dresses and such. He told me he couldn't do it; he couldn't lose another woman he loved. Then he staggered away and left me there with her."

Violet sighed and sat down, taking the bourbon and pressing it into Rita's hands. They were shaking, so Violet helped Rita to drink from the cup, letting her slowly sip it even though she shuddered after each swallow.

"We're going to get Jack and take you home."

"I can't—I can't go there. It…it was her place, and she loved it, and I…can't—" Rita trailed off helplessly and a single tear cut through what remained of the makeup from the night before.

"You'll come to my house," Violet told her. "My maid will ensure you don't drown in the bath, you'll eat some soup or something nour-ishing, and then we'll tuck you into bed."

Another tear chased the first, and Rita asked lamely, "Really? Might I?"

"Of course you will," Violet told her, as though they were longtime friends instead of mere acquaintances.

Violet missed a second chance to view the club, her full attention on leading Rita through to the front. It seemed that the little sympathy and care was enough to send Rita into full tears. Maybe it was exhaus-tion, but Violet knew better. It was realizing that the silly little girl child that Mr. Russell loved was slowly dying.

What a horror and *why?*

Jack took in the scene in a moment and ordered the butler to get a black cab. While they waited, Rita wept on Violet's shoulder, and she slowly rubbed the girl's back. She was a woman, but she felt and seemed like a lost little girl at the moment. Violet channeled her beloved Aunt Agatha and behaved as she thought her aunt might, comforting Rita until the tears stopped.

"Do they know what it was that made her sick?" Jack asked, as he opened the door for Rita and Violet. Rita crawled into the cab and was followed by Violet, who tucked the woman into her side, gently rubbing her hair.

Rita shook her head. "They were discussing it possibly being hemlock. Melody didn't eat anything that would have hemlock in it. Father said she had a piece of boiled roast and bread at dinner and hardly touched any of it. There wasn't anything that could have accidentally been hemlock."

Jack had stiffened, and Violet felt her heart dropping into her stomach. She knew that look. It was the look of a man on the hunt for a killer. Melody might not be dead yet, but she would be soon enough if Rita was correct. Violet closed her eyes against the sight and kept caressing Rita's hair, even though Vi would have preferred to curl into Jack's lap and beg him to say it wasn't so.

They reached Victor's house and took Rita inside. Violet glanced back at Jack. "Don't leave?"

"I'll wait," he said grimly.

Violet took Rita upstairs, encountering Beatrice before reaching her room. Between the two of them, they got Rita bathed, dressed in pajamas, and fed. Rita was nearly asleep before she even hit the pillow. Violet glanced at Beatrice and sighed.

"I know that look, my lady. Is the young woman going to die?"

Violet nodded, not questioning how the maid knew the details. She was sure all of the servants had heard of what happened the previous evening after the odd night with Jack in the house and then the early morning arrival of a doctor and inspector.

Hemlock? Violet shuddered. She had looked into hemlock for a book, as well as having learned of Socrates's death. There wasn't a cure for hemlock. Melody was young so maybe she could pull through, but somehow Violet doubted it. She felt sick as she remembered the trembling, the loss of control, the slow sliding down the ladies room counter onto the floor. And Melody's awareness through it all.

Hemlock poisoning was quite painful. It was a terrible way to die. She hadn't liked Melody Russell, and Violet wouldn't pretend otherwise now. The girl had been grasping and determined to climb as far up the social ladder as the marriage to Mr. Russell would allow. She had gone about her climbing in all the wrong ways and yet had somehow made an intelligent man who had loved before love again.

There had to have been good in Melody Russell, and Violet flinched at her thoughts. Already she was thinking of Mrs. Russell as having died. She hadn't though, had she? She was still battling, trying to stay alive against what had been done to her.

She was going to lose, Violet thought. Without a miracle, Melody Russell would die. Violet pressed her fingers against her temples. She counted to ten, holding her breath until her lungs hurt and then slowly let the air out. Over and over again, she breathed until she no longer felt like crumpling into a heap.

When she looked up, having gathered herself, she saw Jack. He watched her carefully, his penetrating gaze taking everything in. The way her fingers trembled? Certainly. The way her eyes were filled with the imagination of what it might be like to be Melody Russell? That too, of course he saw that. The way Violet's heart was breaking a little more? The way her vision was darkening against the cruelties of this world? The way she ached to protect those she loved and had no idea how to do that?

"I—"

"Do you know why one of the early stories of family in the Bible is of the brothers killing each other?"

Violet slowly shook her head.

"We focus on the wrong things," Jack said, sounding as exhausted and broken as Violet felt. He was letting her see his real feelings, and it made hers all the easier to bear. He was haunted by the vision of Melody Russell as much as Violet, the sick version, the healthy version—they'd seen them both, and what happened was not all right. "They say Eve tempted Adam from the garden, but I think Adam left, following his beloved. Into the wilderness? Fine—wherever she was. To work by the sweat of his brow? Also fine, welcome even. What man doesn't want to work and put a roof over his beloved's head? To create a refuge for his family? We can't keep them perfectly safe, Vi, but even with the tragedy of losing Abel, I think Adam held his wife, shared her tears, and never regretted leaving to be with her."

"So how do they stop weeping?"

"Surely they had other sons and daughters. The ones who loved each other. Who sacrificed for each other. Who adored each other like you and Victor adore one another. They focused on the good. We're so quick to write down the stories of the one brother killing the other. I want to read all the missing good stories. I have to believe they exist."

Violet stepped into his arms, pressing her face against his broad chest, and listened to his heartbeat. She thought that as long as she could hear that song, she could withstand anything. "Or we could just make our own."

"Let's do that too."

"First, though," Violet said fiercely, "let's find this killer."

His kiss on the top of her head was his only answer.

56

CHAPTER 9

*T*he club was deserted when they arrived. The front doors were locked, and Jack had to bang on the door for several minutes before it was opened. Violet recognized the man as one of the waiters from the night before, although he hadn't been their waiter. He glanced them over with a surprise. "Can I help ya?"

"There has been an accident. We need to speak to the staff," Jack said. The guy glanced them over again, taking in Violet, and then his brow furrowed.

"Detective Inspector Wakefield," Jack said, holding out his card. His tone turned into an order. "Now gather everyone up."

They followed the man into the club. Two of the staff were mopping the floor as another two were wiping down tables and arranging chairs. The band was on the stage practicing.

The man who'd let them in gestured to the bar. "Wait here and let me get the manager."

Violet and Jack waited for several minutes, but as they waited staff began to appear around the stage, and the music cut out. Jack led Violet to the stage, and soon the two of them were surrounded by the club's staff, including the hat girl, the waiter from the night before, and others that Violet vaguely recognized but couldn't quite place.

"I'm sure many of you are aware that one of your patrons fell ill yesterday night," Jack told them.

No one spoke, but several people shifted and a few glanced down to the floor.

"I need to speak with everyone who saw her. It's important that we track her evening."

"You were with her the whole time, weren't you?" their waiter demanded.

Vi had quite liked the man the night before, but he was setting her instincts afire with that aggressiveness. She watched as Jack reminded the waiter that Mrs. Russell and her company had been at the club for at least an hour or more before they had shared a table.

"Did anyone serve their party before they joined our table?"

"The two blondes in the same dresses?" the barman asked. He sniffed. "I made them drinks just as they arrived. The shorter one wriggled past everyone and demanded it. Set off quite a few folks."

Jack nodded, glancing around and eyeing all of the staff. "Anyone else?"

Something was nibbling at Violet's memory, but she was distracted from it when the man who ran the club asked, "Why are you asking this? She could have become ill anywhere. You rich folks come in here with things in your pockets and pills and pipes filled with who knows what and then blame us?"

"We're tracking her evening and what she ate," Jack said. "It's as simple as that."

"Why? Did she get some bad shellfish?" the waiter asked.

"You were much nicer last night," Violet told him.

"You were tipping last night."

Violet shrugged at that answer. Jack had over-tipped him more than once for delivering their drinks. Mrs. Russell had become upset time after time that she hadn't received a drink with a rhubarb curl and—Violet blinked rapidly, remembering the three drinks.

"Those were interesting drinks last night," Violet said. "Who came up with the idea for rhubarb and fennel? I thought they were too sour personally, but the others liked them so well."

"You have to come up with new things," the manager said. "They'll order the unusual drink *and* the regular drink if you make it interesting enough." He nodded at his staff. "These are good folks."

"I'm sure they are," Jack said. "Why would they do anything to Mrs. Russell? They'd have no reason, would they?" Jack eyed them in turn.

"Why did Mrs. Russell get the drink without the rhubarb curl three times?" Violet demanded suddenly, staring at the waiter who had served them. "Who put something in that drink and asked you to deliver it?"

The waiter shook his head and stuttered. "I didn't!"

"Just tell us," Violet urged.

Jack had turned on the waiter, and he was focused utterly on him. Vi had never had to experience the full force of those penetrating eyes on her, not like the waiter was, but she'd seen it and she pitied him.

"I didn't," he said again.

"You had a lot of the ready money last night, Teddy," another waiter accused. "More than even a generous table would account for."

The waiter flushed and hissed. "Shut it, Reggie!"

Jack moved so suddenly Violet squeaked. He grabbed the waiter by the lapels and shoved him into the wall. "Did you alter a drink and bring it to the same table *as my female?*"

Violet's brows rose at the words 'my female,' but she kept her reaction to herself as the waiter shook his head frantically. She calmly answered Jack. "Of course he did. Mrs. Russell was the only one who got a different drink. She fell ill soon after we had them. What did you do?" she demanded of the waiter.

"I—" The waiter was trembling, his face so pale, it was ghostly. "I—"

"Out with it, Teddy," the manager said. "Now! Or you won't have to worry about the yard fellow killing you, I'll do it myself."

"The man just had me switch the drinks. I didn't know what it was. He gave me a hundred quid. You know I'm losing my place, Mike. What could I do? He said it wouldn't hurt her."

"Who?" Jack demanded, shaking the waiter. "Who?"

"I don't know! I didn't see his face. It was dark, his hat was low. Big guy, dark hair, nice suit. He said she was his wife, that she was step-ping out on him, and it would make her sleepy—that's all."

"You believed him? You fool!"

"I needed the money," the waiter whined. "He said it wouldn't hurt her!"

"She's dying," Jack told him flatly. "You gave a nineteen-year-old girl a drink with hemlock in it. She's going to die, and it'll be your fault that she does."

"I didn't poison it!"

"Tell that to the judge. One of you boys go get the local bobbie. I don't have time for this fool."

Jack questioned the rest of the staff aggressively to see if anyone else remembered the man. The waiter was crying in the corner, and Jack used him as a reference for the man who had paid to have the poison delivered.

"It wasn't dark hair," the coat girl said. "He had grey hair not brown, but it was a dark grey. If you didn't see it in the light, you might have thought it was brown or black."

One of the cigarette girls agreed and added, "He had a ring. It had a —ah—I'm not sure what you call it. I can draw it."

The manager of the club sent for paper and a pencil.

The cigarette girl drew a double infinity symbol. "It was gold, but the symbol part was black. Kind of spooky looking, thinking back."

Violet prevented her scoff from escaping, but one of the other cigarette girls didn't. Jack lit a cigarette as they took notes on who saw what and were able to narrow down that the second gentlemen who joined Rita and her stepmother had found them at the club. He had seemed to know at least Rita and her date.

Several of the staff had seen Mrs. Russell with the second gentleman in the corner, kissing rather explicitly. Once Mrs. Russell joined Jack and Violet, she hadn't left the table until Rita and Violet had headed to the ladies room.

Violet's head tilted as she considered what she was hearing. The waiter had calmed down and Violet crossed to him, asking gently, "Did you know Mrs. Russell before you brought her that drink?"

He shook his head. His lips trembled. "Do you think I'll hang?"

She had no idea what would happen to him. Had he helped poison a woman? Yes. He hadn't, however, known what he'd been doing. "I think it matters that you were used and didn't realize what would happen."

The poor man nodded frantically. "I wouldn't have done it if I'd known."

"You shouldn't have done it at all," Violet snapped.

He paled again, but he snarled, "What do you know? You're just a spoiled, idiot woman who has no idea what it's like to struggle."

Violet wasn't going to argue with that. She had never been in danger of not having a place to live or food to eat. Her struggles were nothing in comparison to the truly poor, and she knew it too well. She sighed and left the waiter. He'd made a terrible mistake, and he would certainly pay for it to some extent. But his mistake had led a young woman to her impending death, and Violet didn't feel worse for him than she did for Melody Russell.

Jack finished up his questioning and they left the club together.

"I need to talk to Ham about what I found out and be officially assigned to the case. Will you be all right if I take you home?"

Violet nodded. Jack tugged her into an alleyway, tilted her face to his, and kissed her breathless. "You gave Melody Russell your drink, and she offered to trade you. Do you remember? I could have lost you." He kissed her again, and she felt his fingers digging into her spine and the back of her head. "I could have lost you because of that fool and a murderous idiot. I will find this man, and he'll be lucky to survive to reach the prison."

Violet pulled back, just enough to look up at Jack's face. "I'm right here. I'm all right. Nothing happened to me."

"It could have, so easily." Jack shuddered. "Why do the people we love have to be so fragile? By Jove, Vi!"

Violet tangled their fingers together when he finally let go of her and she kissed his jaw. "I don't know why we were so lucky. Given the way Mrs. Russell reacted to her drinks without the rhubarb, we are all quite fortunate that it wasn't more than one of us who succumbed to that poison."

"That's disgustingly true," Jack muttered. "Not that I don't regret Mrs. Russell's outcome. I do, of course."

"It shouldn't have happened at all," Violet agreed, tugging Jack out of the alleyway. "I'll go home and work on my book. Victor and Kate are supposed to leave tomorrow, but I'm sure they'll stay if they need to."

Jack nodded and hailed a black cab. He pulled her body close to his, as if he could protect her from the world by holding her tight. As they motored past their house to Victor's, Jack said, "I'm going to move into our house."

Violet twisted to look at him. "It's not finished. There are workmen there early."

"I'll be staying with you," he said. "Both of our nightmares will ease if I can see you breathe and you can know you aren't alone if you wake."

Violet's eyes widened, but she leaned back into him. She wasn't going to argue. She'd never slept better than when using his shoulder as a pillow and his heartbeat as a lullaby. He deserved an answer, so she said, "Rouge will like that."

Jack laughed and kissed the top of her head in his own response.

CHAPTER 10

*V*iolet was typing away on her story when the door to her bedroom opened and Rita Russell stuck her head in.

"I'm going to the hospital," Rita said. "I wanted to thank you for bringing me to your home and tucking me into bed. You were right. I needed to sleep."

"Do you feel better now?"

Rita was pale and wan, and she shook her head. "She's still going to die, and I feel like there was something I should have done."

"I don't think there was anything we could do," Violet told her. "There isn't a cure for that poison, and we didn't give it to her either way. It was a terrible crime, but it wasn't your crime."

Rita tried to smile, but she failed at it. She was still wearing Violet's pajamas and kimono. "My poor Papa. I need to go. He needs me. I'll either go back to the house with him or to the hotel, but thank you for seeing to me."

Violet nodded. "Did you want to borrow something to wear so you can go straight to the hospital?"

Rita took in a slow breath. "Yes, I was hoping you'd let me."

Violet dug through the closet, fighting the desire to ask Rita about the double infinity symbol and interfering in Jack's case. She pulled out a dress that she didn't mind bidding adieu. Violet handed the dress over, found Rita stockings, and let her leave to dress. They weren't even close to the same size in shoes, so Rita was going to have to wear her evening shoes.

Violet went down to the parlor and called for tea. It was late in the afternoon, and she wanted to curl up with a plate of sandwiches and biscuits and set herself afloat on a sea of tea. She set herself up with a sketchbook and drew several version of a double infinity symbol and placed them in ready view.

When Rita appeared, Violet asked, "Would you like tea before you go?"

"Oh," she said, her gaze lingering on the food. "I am famished."

Violet waved Rita in and poured her tea. Having sent Hargreaves to warn Victor and Kate to keep scarce, they were alone for the tea.

"Are you sketching?" Rita asked, leaning forward after taking a long sip of tea.

"Working on something for my book. I saw a ring with this symbol on it, and I thought it would work well for this secret society in my story."

"What a funny idea," Rita said, frowning at it. "I've seen that symbol somewhere before. I—think I've seen it on a ring, too."

"Have you?" Violet said. "Perhaps we both saw the same person. It's a small world, isn't it?"

Rita shook her head, frowning deeply as she stared. "It seems like it has been a while, however, since I saw it. Perhaps I saw it when I was in Africa? No," she mused. "India. I am almost positive it was India."

Violet leaned back. "India? Are you certain?"

"Yes." Rita nodded. "How funny to think back. That was the last time I was truly happy. Mother was alive, and we were seeing the most amazing things around the country. Father worked while Mother and I experienced the most diverse and unique offerings of the country. We'd return home and eat this mix of Indian and English food. I just loved it there. I rode an elephant and ate hot peppers that made me cry. I had a little monkey. It was wonderful. Then mother died, and we returned home to England, and everything was grey. I left again but never quite found the same joy."

Violet wanted to shake Rita to turn her attention back to the symbol, but Rita had adjusted her mind somewhere else, and Violet wasn't sure it was a good idea to draw Rita's attention to a clue that Jack was pursing.

Rita left soon after, and Violet hauled up the stairs to find Victor and Kate. Her brother demanded, "Are we allowed to eat now?"

The small table in their bedroom was covered with a tea tray, an empty sandwich tray, and a few remaining petit fours. Violet smacked his arm. "I was prying. You'd have loved it, but, of course, you weren't invited. Your home or not."

"Darling Vi," Kate interrupted, rubbing her growing belly. "Will you be all right if we leave in a few days?"

"We have to have a house for that thing you're growing," Victor told Kate. "Therefore, Denny is prepared to shuck off the fetters of his laziness and protect our Violet. Jack also said there's no reason to believe that Violet would be a target for this killer. I'd have to agree. Vi barely knows these people."

"Miss Allen and Isolde sent Rita my way," Violet told him. "We should have Isolde over to dinner before you go. Isolde can come chaperone me," Violet suggested. "And perhaps help distract Lady Eleanor. I do wish Father would handle our stepmother."

Victor laughed sarcastically. "Father isn't in London to stop Lady Eleanor from destroying your engagement. He trusts Jack a little and me a little more. Father is here to stand guard over Isolde's already stolen virtue."

"Does he know it's gone?" Violet asked.

"Is it really gone?" Kate asked. "Is it fair even to focus on Isolde's virtue? What about Tomas? Or this animal, Victor? What truly determines virtue or the lack thereof?"

"Oh, I agree with you, Kate." Violet held up her hands. "Jack chose to abide by the traditional thoughts on virtue without consulting me, and I haven't argued because I would rather Father liked him, especially given Lady Eleanor's character."

"As would I," Victor inserted. "But for Jack, this isn't about his opinion of you, Vi, or whether your virtue is intact or not. He's protecting you."

"Jack," Violet told them, taking one of the seats near the table, "took a waiter at the club by the lapels, slammed him into the wall, and shook him like a dog for, and I quote him here, 'Bringing an altered drink to the same table *as his female.*'"

Victor's choked laughter turned into a deep cough and Violet winked at Kate while they watched Victor struggle to breathe.

"That's a winner of a man you have there," Violet told Kate.

She reached out and rubbed her husband's shoulder. "Yes, I know."

"How is my Vi junior?"

"She's good," Kate told Violet. "Will you really be all right if we leave you for a few days? Victor won't be calm until he has a place to put over this baby's head."

"Yes," Violet said simply. "Jack is determined to keep me by his side."

Victor curled onto his side, placing his head on his wife's lap. "What does that mean?"

"I think you know the answer to that," Violet replied.

"Father is going to kill me." Victor wiped his eyes and sat up. "Everything is less amusing now."

"Whatever are you afraid of with Father? That he'll cut you off? He won't. Not for something I do."

"He told me that he would drag me on a family vacation with him and make both Geoffrey and Lady Eleanor come. Father *knows* Geoffrey is a wart."

Violet had to bite the inside of her mouth to hold back her gasp and control her voice to a lazy idleness. "Father threatened you with his wife?"

"He knows she's a wart too," Victor said. "Not that he said so. But his threat made it all clear enough. You want to know why Father is such a good shot? He goes shooting to escape Lady Eleanor. No wonder men have clubs. They realize what they've married and have to hide. When you add in young blighters like our brother, Geoffrey, well, you'd almost feel sorry for Father."

"Except," Violet said and was joined in by Kate, "He married her."

"Just so," Victor added with the same lack of sympathy. "Saddled all of us with her. Kate protects me now when she doesn't abandon me."

"It's hard enough to eat or breathe with your devil spawn pushing on my lungs," Kate told Victor. "Kicking me in the ribs. Making it impossible to see my feet. I hardly need to add in your stepmother."

JACK DID NOT APPEAR for dinner or for evening cocktails and listening to the wireless. Violet read over her earlier work in a chair near the fire, making notes on the pages and handing them over to her brother. He'd take care of the editing and adding in a spooky atmosphere. He did spooky so much better than she did, but she did the emotional part for them both.

Violet frowned as she took a deep breath in and washed her face. She had little doubt Jack would appear sooner or later since he'd said he would. She'd have liked to speak to him about the conversation with Rita. Could what Rita had seen as a younger woman in India have anything to do with Mrs. Russell's impending death or was it simply a coincidence?

She put on pajamas that covered her completely and then her kimono. Violet journaled for a while, looking back over her recent grey days and trying to determine if anything had caused them. She went from there to scratching Rouge's belly, talking to the dog.

Victor stuck his head into the room. "Leave your door open."

"Lady Eleanor is coming for you regardless of what Jack and I do or don't do. Father wouldn't threaten you with time with her and Geoffrey if it wasn't on his mind."

"My door will also be open should he appear."

"Uh oh." Violet's smirk had Victor shooting her a daggered glance, but those had little effect on the woman who'd shared a womb with him. He'd have to save them for their younger sister Isolde or their ward Ginny. "Make sure you choose a room for Ginny in whatever house you buy and tell her about it."

"She's going to have more bedrooms across the whole of England than a princess," Victor countered, "but I will. I ordered her some chocolates from that place you went as well. Sent it along with a few quid and a new coat Kate bought her."

"Good. It's important she knows we love her when the baby comes. She isn't confident enough in us as it is."

"She's a good kid." Victor entered the room and dropped a kiss on Vi's head. "You'll be careful whether we're here or not."

"Always."

"I'm tired of people dying." He ruffled her hair, deliberating messing up what she'd just straightened. "Leave the door open."

"You know," Violet called when he was nearly gone, "what the best part of you having a baby is?"

"The baby?"

"Introducing Lady Eleanor as grandmother."

Victor's eyes widened with sheer joy, and they grinned at each other with the same evil smirks. "Oh, Violet," he breathed. "You've made my entire year, darling sister. My entire year."

He pushed her door open a little more, put a shoe in front of it so it wouldn't blow closed, and winked at her lifted brow.

Violet fell asleep shortly after and woke again possibly minutes, possibly hours later when Jack pulled her into his arms.

"Is all well?" she whispered, still half asleep.

"Mrs. Russell died an hour ago," Jack said. "It is officially murder."

Violet snuggled into his side, placing her hand over his chest to feel the movement of his breath.

"Are you all right?" She rubbed her chin against his chest as she waited for him to answer.

A long while later he did. "No. But holding you helps."

Violet fell back asleep, but she wasn't sure that Jack slept at all when he rose the next morning before she did and slipped out of the house and down the street to their new home.

CHAPTER 11

*V*iolet dressed for the day with the assumption she'd be staying home. She had her jiu jitsu lesson, took a long, lingering bath, walked with Rouge and Victor's dog, Gin, in the garden. They walked down to the house she would move into after she married and looked at the updates. Victor had given her some of the paintings from the house he'd bought while drunk. They'd sold the house and kept the abandoned family portraits. It appealed to both of their senses of humor to keep the other family's portraits rather than abandon them to the garbage.

In her new house, the paper was up on the walls and the house smelled of paint from the freshly redone walls and ceilings. The newly refinished floors shone so brightly the sun reflected from the windows. Mr. Cuthbert, the butler, contained his reaction to see the muddy little dogs, and Violet had to hand it to the man that he handled the dogs well. He sent one of the daily maids to the kitchens with the dogs and led her through the house to show her the updates that had been done since her last visit.

She found Jack's man in the bedroom, hanging his clothes. The house was one of those old-style houses that had a room for the lady of the house as well as the man of the house. It hadn't been updated to remove the connecting door, and Jack and Violet had decided to keep it. Though they still intended to share a bedroom.

"My lady," Nevin, Jack's man, said, "Mr. Jack said you used the closet in the next room."

Violet grinned and admitted, "I have too many clothes to share a closet, my good man. And on occasion, I write until the early hours. My typewriter and clothing will be in the adjoining room."

"Do you need anything, my lady? Mr. Jack has gone to work."

Violet shook her head. "I'm here to see the updates. I think now that I've seen the walls for the second bedroom that I'll wander the furniture warehouses to look for the right set for me."

He nodded, and she left him to Jack's wardrobe. Jack really had moved in, Violet saw. She'd almost expected him to change his mind when they had a little distance from realizing how easily they could have lost each other.

It was a thrill to walk through her future house. Some of the rooms were entirely empty still, and Violet felt a bit of pressure to complete the purchases.

As she maneuvered through the house with Mr. Cuthbert discussing the things yet slated to be completed, Violet asked him, "Are you ready for a party yet, Mr. Cuthbert?"

His eyes widened with even more alarm than the muddy dogs had caused. "Whenever you need, my lady," he told her.

She nodded once. "Perhaps not quite yet."

She ignored his relief, gathered the dogs from the maid and returned to Victor's house. As she walked up the steps a boy walked down them, and he nodded and ran off. Violet found that the boy had left a card for her inviting her to the Piccadilly Ladies Club for lunch with Rita and a few other members. Violet's mouth twisted. Rita had just lost her stepmother, even if it was a girl Rita had half-hated. Violet wasn't so sure it was the best choice to go to the luncheon.

She already knew, however, she would go. Violet had to hurry if she wasn't going to be too late. She found Beatrice putting dresses away.

"Find me something, ah, fashionable, clearly rich, and daring, but appropriate for luncheon."

Beatrice's gaze widened as Violet dropped onto the stool at her vanity and hurried through her makeup. She finished with an apple red lipstick. The dress Beatrice selected was grey with simple lines that accented Violet's slim figure. The power of it was in the grey on grey embroidery, which reflected an attention to detail and expense that few could match.

Violet examined her jewelry. "The black pearls, Lady Violet," Beatrice suggested. "If you're going to a ladies club, many of them will have traditional pearls, but the excessive set that your brother bought you—no one else has that. Not even Mrs. Kate."

That was a telling point, Violet thought as she put on her necklace. Victor really needed to top for his wife what he'd given Violet. She added diamond and pearl earbobs and several bracelets. She normally wouldn't have worn quite so much jewelry for a luncheon, but she was putting on a persona.

Violet added a pretty, grey cloche and then a coat with fur trim. The ladies club was filled with the type of women she thought she might like. What concerned her wasn't the women there or the embedded snobbishness that would invite Violet but not someone like Ginny—at least before Ginny became Violet's ward. What concerned Violet was that Rita Russell had lost her stepmother the night previous and today she was asking an earl's daughter to a social event.

It had been evident from the beginning of their association that Violet's father's title had mattered to Miss Russell. Why though? When it had been an excuse to avoid inviting Melody Russell to the club, perhaps, it made sense. The problem was why now. Was it the earl? Violet was afraid that it was not. She was very much afraid that it was Jack who had Rita Russell reaching out again.

She left a note for Jack for if he returned, checked in with her brother, and left for the ladies club in a black cab. The drive through London was dreary with the January rain and the thick clouds. Violet hurried up the stairs to the club when the clouds opened and poured out. She had been so busy adjusting her makeup and her dress, she hadn't prepared with an umbrella.

She opened the door without waiting and nodded at the same butler she had met the day previous. Violet breathed out, shook her head a little and accepted the towel that the butler provided, following her to the ladies room to freshen.

Her makeup had been destroyed by the rain, so Violet's mouth twisted and she wiped her face clean—carefully avoiding her drawn-on eyebrows—then shrugged. If Jack loved her freckles, Violet would too. She reapplied her lipstick, used the towel on her feet and shoes, and then exited the room.

The butler was waiting for Violet when she exited the ladies room. "Miss Russell is waiting for you with a few others."

Violet nodded and followed the butler to the dining room. There were small tables around a very large room and at least two-thirds of the tables were full. The food smelled divine, and Violet could see the appeal of having a lunch with women of a like mind. Perhaps she would truly join the ladies club after all.

Violet was brought to the table where Miss Russell was seated with another woman who was quite a bit older. Violet had thought that Rita Russell had looked like her father when she'd seen the woman, but now she could see that she took after this woman.

"Lady Violet," Rita said, as Violet took the seat that was held for her. "May I introduce you to my aunt, Mrs. Jean Albright."

Violet shook hands with the woman. She was brought water as they commented on the weather.

Finally, Rita spoke. "I suppose you heard?"

Violet nodded and waited. She wasn't going to broach this subject for Rita. Not even if Violet couldn't help but like her. The woman glanced at her aunt and back at Violet. "It's shocking, I know, to invite you to lunch after she died. I—I should be home with my father, but he doesn't want me there. It seems the daughter of his first wife—who made her feelings clear about the second wife—isn't so welcome while he's mourning her. He did, however, charge me with talking to you."

"To me?"

"While we waited for her to...pass—well, I told him what I'd heard of you. I was only talking randomly because I didn't know what to say or do, but it seems he was listening."

Violet's brows lifted, and she sipped the water that had been placed in front of her. They ordered a few moments later and while they did, Rita avoided Violet's gaze. Regardless, eventually the waitress disappeared with their order and Rita was forced to explain.

"He wants you to help find Melody's killer. He says she was robbed of her life and you have stepped in for women like her before."

Violet leaned back, unsurprised by the request. Being involved with Jack's cases, combined with her family connections, had added an allure to her interfering that was far more romantic than it deserved. This avenging angel earl's daughter who stepped in for the victims. The person who deserved the respect was Jack, but Violet was too unusual being a lady and an heiress not to steal the recognition for solving cases simply by being odd.

"You can be assured," Violet told them both, "that Jack is more than capable and will do all that is possible to be done for your family."

"My father will be comforted if you say yes."

Mrs. Albright shifted, and Violet could tell by the woman's expression that she was not nearly as comfortable with the request as Rita. To be fair, however, Violet had to acknowledge the blush on the woman's cheeks. Her tanned skin hid it a little better than Violet's fair skin would have, but it was there if you could acknowledge it.

"Mrs. Albright," Violet said, without answering Rita, "are you the aunt who traveled India with Rita after they lost her mother?"

The woman nodded.

"Are you familiar with a double infinity symbol?" Violet asked.

She nodded again. "Of course. It's hardly all unique."

"Are you working on your book right now?" Rita's dismay was clear as day, but Violet ignored her.

"Rita told me she'd seen it on a ring? On a gold ring? With black etching to make the symbol?"

"Well, yes, of course," Mrs. Albright answered. "Her father, my husband, and several of their friends wore them after school and for years—it took a while before they truly stopped. I don't think I've seen them for some time."

Oh, Violet thought, biting her lip. Jack needed to know. He might already know if he'd asked Mr. Russell about it, but...Violet excused herself and found the butler. "I must make a telephone call immediately."

Violet was shown to a room and was able to reach Hamilton Barnes. Jack was working in the city, so Violet explained everything and Hamilton listened, taking notes before he asked, "Are you safe?"

"Of course I am," Violet told him. "I'm at that ladies club where we found Miss Russell and am having lunch with her. I expect I'll return to the house just after."

"Do," Hamilton ordered and then added, "Violet, it's important that you're safe. That's the most important thing to Jack."

"It's a *ladies* club, Ham," she laughed. "I think I'll be safe enough. Whoever poisoned Mrs. Russell was a man, and they aren't welcome here. I'll go straight home, shall I?"

"Please," Ham said, adding almost sheepishly, "I really have no way of arresting my best friend for murder, so I'm going to need nothing to happen to you. Really ever, Violet."

CHAPTER 12

"I promise I will do all I can," Violet told Rita as they left the ladies club. They were going to share a cab, and as they approached it, there was a loud crack. After the space of a heartbeat, Violet reacted instinctively, grabbing Miss Russell and throwing them both to the ground, and also tried to find the car that was backfiring.

There was, however, another loud crack and the glass on the black cab exploded, raining down over the two women. Rita was screaming, but Violet had gone into a sort of tunnel vision and automatic reaction, sliding closer to the shadow of the auto, hauling Rita with her to hide behind the metal. The glass had sprayed over them, Violet reasoned, so the bullets were coming from the other side.

People were screaming, but Violet cared for nothing but the safety of the auto protecting her. Rita had gone nearly as quiet as Violet. The two of them were clutching each other as if the other was a life raft and they were at sea.

The shooting stopped. Rita's gaze focused on Violet's

"Someone was shooting at us." Rita said what Violet was thinking. Someone had been *shooting* at them. Outside of the ladies club. A ladies club! In London! *Why?*

A few minutes later, a local constable knelt in front of them. "The shooter is gone, ladies. You're all right now. Let's get inside, shall we?" His voice was low and gentle, and his eyes were wide with concern. Violet could see that he was a good man just by the expression on his face.

Violet shook her head over and over again, and she glanced up as she heard a man shouting, "Out of the way." She knew that voice, though she had never heard such a bellow from it.

People stumbled to the side from the force of something behind them, and then Jack burst through the edge of the onlookers.

He reached down, ignoring Rita, and hauled Violet into his arms and carried her up the steps of the ladies club. When they reached the inside, Jack brushed the glass off of Violet. They were, the both of them, shaking.

"How did you know?" Violet asked, as he picked the glass off of her. She cared nothing for the crowd of onlookers. She wrapped her arms around his waist, pressed her face into his chest and breathed slowly in and out. It wasn't enough. She tried to listen to him, but really all she wanted was the surety that she was alive.

"I talked to the waiter from the club again this morning. I wanted a moment by moment detail of what he'd been told, how he got the adjusted drinks, all of it."

"What was he told?" Rita had arrived, although Violet hadn't noticed. She cracked her eyes open and looked at the woman, who had her arms wrapped around herself. Her aunt had left before Violet and Rita, and she seemed to be alone in the horror of what she was experiencing. Violet didn't let go of Jack, but she held out a hand to Rita, who took it.

"To give it to the flashy blonde in the black dress." Jack shook his head against the top of Violet's. "I realized that Rita was blonde too, and they were wearing the same dress. I told Hamilton we should check on Rita, and he said you were here, with her. I just...*knew?* I don't know. Maybe I simply worried and it was luck. If nothing had happened, I suppose I would assume I was overreacting."

"But something did happen," she said for him. Violet took in a shuddering breath. There was a crowd of women watching both them and Rita, who was shaking nearly as hard as Violet, their hands clutched together.

"Why would someone try to kill me?" Rita asked, her lips trembling, and Violet could see the fear hitting her. She might rally later and be the fierce, independent woman that she was, but it would come after she got through these moments.

Violet answered her honestly. "Love, hatred, greed, jealousy, revenge, they're simply mad. We'll figure it out and stop it."

Rita's gaze narrowed on Violet and her expression was fierce. "That didn't save Melody."

"We didn't know anyone was trying to hurt you or her." Jack released Violet but kept his hand on her back as if he couldn't quite let go completely. "We can't save everyone, but we can try. You, however, I don't see why we can't save you."

"She can come to Victor's house," Violet told him. His jaw clenched, and she could see his desire to instantly say no. He didn't argue, but she knew he might later. That was fine, she'd let him decide. She didn't want to be a casualty in another person's war, and she had little doubt that Jack would do what he could for Rita while protecting Violet.

"Is this what life is like for you, Lady Violet?" one of the women asked. "Someone push her membership through."

Several of the women laughed while Violet watched Jack barely hold back a furious scold.

Violet winked merrily, although it was all false, and finished shaking the glass from her hair and dress. "I'm a package deal, you know?" Violet told them. "There's no ladies club without my own friends."

One of the women nodded and another muttered, "Cheeky."

Violet ignored them both, hardly caring if the Piccadilly Ladies Club made her a member or asked her never to return.

She took off her coat and tried shaking it out. The butler, however, took it from Violet, along with Rita's coat, and promised to brush them both most carefully.

"Where shall we go?" Violet asked Jack. "If we take Rita to Victor's house—"

Jack shook his head. "Is your father home alone?" he asked Rita.

With a quick negative, Rita added, "Father's friends and family have been appearing all day. I'd have been there myself but for my mission from Father. I'm sure my aunt, who was with us, has returned already. I had intended to stop by the hotel where my things are and pack a bag, perhaps even move home."

"Not yet," Jack told her. "Don't move home yet at all. Violet—" He winced before finishing his thought. "What about your father's house? You'll be close enough for Rita to be readily accessible to her father while also having more servants than the rest of us, and all of them reliable."

"No," Violet and Rita said in unison. Their gazes met.

Rita stammered. "I can't...Lady Eleanor...I—I'm sorry, Violet, but I can't."

"I agree," Violet told Jack. "Victor's servants are all reliable and other *things* will be easier."

Jack studied her, knowing she was referring to them sleeping together. They were *only* sleeping together, but Violet never intended to sleep without him if it was possible. She hadn't had a nightmare in the last two days despite all of the fodder for them. She was going sleep in Jack's arms if she had to hike through London, find him, and make him hold her.

They were shown to a small room while Jack called the yard and Violet and Rita stared at each other.

"Is it like this for you often?"

"That was alarming in the extreme. You must have been in alarming situations before," Violet said. "A tiger while you were in India or a lion in Africa?"

"There was the most horrible snake in Africa," Rita admitted. "And another in India. I almost died because I froze. Like today."

"I recognize the sound of gunshots because my father is a very good shot and shoots nearly every day in the country. My body knew what it was before my mind had caught up."

Rita's mouth twisted. "I've never been much of a hunter. Father either."

"Have you ever been engaged?" Violet asked, seemingly randomly but with her own purpose. A jilted lover, perhaps?

Rita hesitated, then admitted, "I've been asked a few times, but I've always declined. I've never been sure they wanted *me* and not Father's money."

"Is your father's money going to be your money?"

The girl paused a long time and then slowly nodded. "I'd expect so. I've never had reason to believe that Father wouldn't leave me the money."

"If something happens to you," Violet asked, "who would get the money?"

"Father has two siblings. One or both of them, I'd suspect."

"What about enemies? Do you have those? Or your father?"

Rita shrugged helplessly. "Father made rather a lot of money. I suspect there are always enemies in business when that much money is involved. I don't think anyone would hate me enough to kill me. Though I'm not to everyone's taste, you know? Independent, wanting to travel and explore and experience rather than settle down and have children. I've had lovers. Maybe what seemed like an amiable parting wasn't?" Rita shrugged helplessly again.

"Someone wants you dead for some reason." Violet glanced around the small office and then back at Rita.

"What a funny thing to think," Rita mused, not sounding amused in the slightest. "Someone wants me dead. They almost killed me, but for the mistake of that waiter, I'd be the one who had succumbed to hemlock and died that horrible death. She couldn't speak, but you could see she was in pain. It was a terrible way to die."

Violet nodded and rose, pacing the room and playing with her engagement ring. She felt like she needed her journal and a chalkboard. Something to write on while she pinned down who might have an advantage if Rita died.

One of the women from the club came in with a teapot, and both

Violet and Rita looked at it too long. "I swear I didn't poison it," the woman said, holding up her hands. "I can understand your concern."

"Why would you, Marguerite? We're just spooked, I think."

"The president told me to ask Lady Violet what the names were of 'her ladies?'"

Violet frowned from where she was pacing. "Ginny Holmes, Lila Lancaster, Kate Carlyle, and Isolde Carlyle."

The woman nodded and left as quietly as she came. Both Violet and Rita looked again at the tea, and then Violet admitted, "I'm not drinking it."

"She wouldn't poison us. She doesn't know me well enough to want to kill me."

"She'd be a fool if she did. Jack wouldn't arrest her, he'd strangle her with his bare hands."

Rita smoothed her hands lightly over her hair. Violet could tell that her thoughts had shifted. "It must be nice to have someone love you so much. Now that I have calmed down, the sight of him storming through the crowd and hauling you out of the glass and to safety was, perhaps, the most romantic thing I have ever seen."

Violet wasn't sure how to respond to any of that. She hadn't seen romance, she'd seen agony in his eyes. The way he'd been so sure he'd lost her. The relief when he realized she was all right and then the fury, the stark, raving fury, at whomever had put her at risk. Nothing about that was romantic to Violet.

"Who doesn't want to be loved?" was her only reply.

CHAPTER 13

*J*ack returned to the small office while Violet was pacing. He took her in and said, "I've spoken to Ham, Mr. Russell, and Victor. We will be going to Victor's house, and he'll be bringing in Denny and Lila."

Violet's mouth twitched at the certain glee Denny would experience when they gathered around another chalkboard and discussed the suspects. Jack's gaze glinted with a similar amusement that faded into a nearly untranslatable darkness.

"Before we go to the house, we'll be stopping by Mr. Russell's home. He has a houseful of friends and family who need to see and speak with Miss Russell."

Violet didn't scoff at Jack's lie. Mr. Russell had a house full of suspects. If someone was going to profit by the attempted murder, they were almost certainly in the house. Otherwise, it was an enemy, and Jack would need to speak in detail with Mr. Russell about who might despise him enough to murder his wife and his daughter.

"Ham will be meeting us there," Jack told Violet. "While I talk to Mr. Russell about this business, Ham will stay with you."

"Who is Ham?" Rita asked, as Jack held out her coat for her to put on.

"A good friend. After the events of the day, I'll need someone I trust with eyes on Violet while I work."

"See," Rita smiled almost jealously, "romantic."

Entrapment, Violet thought, but she smiled and let Jack help her into her own coat. Hamilton Barnes, Jack's boss. A quiet, rotund man with the same penetrating gaze as Jack and the same ability to follow the thoughts of a criminal through the dregs of society. Eyes on Violet? Yes. Certainly, Ham was the only person outside of Victor that Jack would entrust with Violet's safety. He wasn't there just for that, however. He was there to watch the people in the guise of lamb without them ever realizing he was a wolf.

"Hamilton is being motored over by a local constable and then he'll take us to Mr. Russell's home. Victor said he'd meet us there with his own auto and Hargreaves to take you and Miss Russell home."

Rita listened without further questions, and Violet didn't explain what was actually happening. They were using the grief and shock of the Russell family to ferret out a murderer.

Jack sent Rita with the constable before Violet, and Vi had little doubt it had been done deliberately. If the shooter had returned, he wouldn't get Violet when he tried for Rita. Nothing happened, but Jack waited for several long minutes before he walked Violet to the auto. Even after waiting, he kept her behind him the entire short distance.

"I object as strenuously to something happening to you as you do to me," she told his back.

Jack glanced at her, and he smiled just with his eyes. "I'm larger than you. I can take more damage than you."

Violet didn't agree, but she knew if it came down to it, he'd physi-cally haul her to whatever seemed to be safest to him. They slid into a second police car, and Jack greeted the driver before pulling Violet directly into his side. He settled his chin over the top of her head and murmured, "I think we must have the worst luck in all of London."

Violet shook her head under his chin. "We have each other, money, a nice home, love, and we weren't the ones who drank the poison. We do, however, have pretty bad luck when it comes to our associations."

"We know too many killers," Jack agreed.

"It's your fault," they said in unison.

Jack pulled back so he could see Violet's face and then tilted her mouth to his. He stole her breath with his lips. He set her on fire, and she wanted nothing more than to climb into his lap. The sound of traffic, the awareness of the constable behind the wheel, everything but Jack faded until she pulled away and pressed her face into his neck to catch her breath.

"Jack," she whispered against his skin, and he placed his hand against her lower back, holding her tight against his side.

"Violet," he told her, "after this case and Victor and Kate buying their house, we're going somewhere where we know no one, and we're going to walk, sleep, and read books."

She laid her head on his shoulder. "It doesn't take that long to get to somewhere warmer. A good steamship, a few days, and then we can spend days in the sun."

The auto pulled onto the earl's street and to the Russell mansion. They walked to the house and were let inside. Violet nodded at the butler, who had the same impassive face, but this time there was nothing humorous in his gaze.

"Miss Rita," he said as they entered. "Are you well?"

Rita nodded, but no one believed her.

"Mr. Wakefield, Mr. Russell asked me to bring you to his office. Everyone else is gathered the parlor. Miss Rita, your father wants you to join him as well."

Violet and Ham followed the butler to a parlor to join Mrs. Albright and several other men and women more of her age than Rita's. Mrs. Albright, the sister of the first Mrs. Russell who had died years before, seemed familiar with the others. She appeared almost cozy despite the solemnity of the situation.

There were four men, two women, and a vicar beyond Mrs. Albright. There was also a clear division in the room. As Violet was introduced, she categorized them mentally versus trying to remember their names individually. The men were all linked to Mr. Russell, though they didn't appear to share the same side. She had the brothers, older and younger, the business partner, and the long-time friend. They each had solemn faces and every single one of the men was tall enough and grey enough to be the person who had arranged for Mrs. Russell's poisoning. Could one of them have been the shooter as well?

"They couldn't make it easy for us, could they?" Hamilton asked.

One of the two women was Mrs. Russell's sister, who stood speaking with the vicar, with the business partner nearby. The other men and final woman grouped on the other side of the parlor. The two brothers were talking quietly together as the long-time friend looked on. Mrs. Albright was fluttering about as if she were the hostess of a gathering. The last woman sat alone sipping from a cup of tea.

Violet and Ham watched the groups. "This is terribly awkward," Violet murmured. "Shall we slide our way in?"

"We need names and histories," Ham told Violet. "Who served in the armed forces or who is an expert marksman? That shot taken at you today was risky, but no one would try that if they weren't confident in their skillset."

"Perhaps that will be enough. You know, I have an idea," Violet told him. "I need to leave here, however, and I think you'll need to remain."

"Do you want Jack to rip me apart piece by piece?"

"Ham," Violet said, glancing around the parlor, "I'm going to gossip with the servants."

His gaze sharpened with interest. "I will murder you myself if you get hurt."

"No, you won't," Violet told him. "Keep them in here, if you can."

Hamilton led Violet to the door, ensuring no one followed, and Violet wandered across the beautiful black and white tiles back the way she came until she found the man she'd been hunting.

"Hullo," she said. "Just who I was looking for."

His impassive face did not adjust in the slightest. "Oh?"

Violet grinned for a moment. "I'm going to say things that shouldn't be overheard."

His eyebrows lifted just a bit at that and then he silently led the way to a small office barely larger than a closet. "How may I help you, Lady Violet?"

"Someone is trying to kill Miss Russell," Violet told him flatly. "They poisoned Mrs. Russell by accident and then they shot at Miss Russell today as she was leaving the ladies club."

"I've heard," the man said slowly, still even and guarded in his expression.

"I need your help," Violet told him, low and quiet as if they could be overhead. "Servants know everything. Who is the heir?"

"Miss Russell is," the butler said after a long moment. "After seeing to longtime servants or small bequests to friends."

"What happens to the money if Miss Russell dies first?"

The butler shook his head. "That wasn't accounted for in the will."

"Those brothers are the only living family of Mr. Russell?"

He nodded.

"Are either of them good shots? Perhaps extraordinarily so?"

"No, my lady," he said. "I believe that the younger Mr. Russell is very much known to be clumsy. He also has quite terrible eyesight. The older Mr. Russell has bad gout and a bad heart.

Violet sighed and muttered, "I suppose that is too easy." She eyed the butler, and he eyed her in return, seeming to want to tell her something but not quite putting it out into the air. "Who do you suspect?"

"It doesn't make sense," the man told her.

Violet wasn't worried about sense at the moment. She was worried about who was doing the killing and why.

"Why?"

"All of the men have been here most of the day. If the shooter was intending to kill Miss Rita—"

"He was," Violet told the butler clearly.

"Then the shooter was hired."

Violet held in a sigh of frustration. She was getting nowhere. "Is there anything else you can tell me?"

"Only that I wouldn't leave a small child in the same room as Mrs.

Albright," the butler said. For once an expression crossed his face and it was one of utter disgust. "She's just evil."

"Evil?"

Violet considered the luncheon she'd had with the woman earlier that day and couldn't quite see it. She had, if anything, seemed clingy and weak.

"You don't agree," he said. She didn't respond and he would say nothing more, so she followed the butler back to the parlor. Hamilton was already in the hall and Jack was exiting the office where he and Rita had met with Mr. Russell. Jack frowned in her direction when he realized she was returning from somewhere unescorted except for the butler.

"One of the boys showed up here," Hamilton told Jack and Violet as they joined him. "We need to confer and perhaps get Miss Russell somewhere safe."

"I am not trying to hurt my daughter," Mr. Russell argued. "I don't like this plan of taking her away."

"I can only imagine how you must feel, Mr. Russell," Jack told him, and by his tone he'd said this more than one time. "The person who tried to harm your daughter knew where she'd be and when she'd be there. The last time I dealt with someone who refused to seek refuge to avoid the clear attempts on her life, she didn't survive."

Violet bit down on her bottom lip hard. Very hard. That had been her great aunt, the woman who had raised Vi. Her greatest regret was being unable to convince her aunt to hide until the culprit was located.

Mr. Russell met Jack's gaze and nodded. "All right. All right. Take good care of my baby. She's all I have."

"We will," Jack promised, holding out his hand. "As I have said before, I will find the culprit. Twice now, they almost took all I have from me."

"Hold her tight," Mr. Russell said, sounding exhausted. "You don't get over losing someone you love. No matter what lies the world would tell you."

CHAPTER 14

"*I*s it time?" Denny demanded. He waved Violet into the parlor and she shook her head at him.

Hargreaves was waiting in the hallway, and Violet could see beyond the open door to the familiar chalkboard. Denny had already titled it with "Suspects," leaving room for the notes and questions she wrote out. She lifted her brows at him and he grinned. "I have chocolate."

"I was shot at, dear Denny. I feel I must scrub my hair and skin to ensure all the glass is off of me. Otherwise I shall have some fall into my soup."

He started to object, but the sight of both Victor and Jack behind Violet must have been enough to silence him. With a bit of a whiny frown, he said, "We're ready when you are. I'd have ordered in dinner for us all, but Hargreaves said we do not eat food that we don't prepare ourselves. They're scurrying around the kitchens to make us something."

"I'm sure whatever they made will be fine," Violet told him. "Cook is a professional."

Denny, Lila, and Kate were dressed for dinner already. Kate's gaze was worried but clear, and she still seemed to glow, so Violet didn't worry that today's near-miss had upset her sister-in-law too much.

If not for the guests, Violet would just as soon have put on her pajamas and avoided food entirely, but she could see that wasn't going to happen. Denny had that look of glee and joy in his eye that said he'd never rest until he was able to list out the suspects and discuss the puzzle of the crime. Unlike Violet and Jack, who were haunted by crimes, Denny seemed entertained. He wasn't really. He was a good man for all his laziness, but he wasn't bothered by the things that didn't immediately affect him.

"I hear you've been shopping, Vi," Denny said with a smirk.

Violet's gaze shot to Lila, who had gasped and slapped her husband's arm.

"I—" Lila started.

"Don't make me set Jack and Victor on you, Denny my lad," Violet told him. "Both of them are feeling very protective." She noticed Rita standing at the edge of the group and gestured her closer. "I'm sure you wish to give yourself a good scrub too, Rita," Violet said after introductions. "Our adventure today was one to leave your skin crawling with the certainty that something remains behind no matter how many times we brush off our skin and hair."

"It did," Rita agreed. Her bright blue eyes flicked amongst the friends. "What a lovely chosen family you have. I suppose that is the biggest problem to traveling nearly incessantly. You don't have friend-ships like the ones I sense here."

"Have you really been to Africa?" Denny asked.

Rita nodded.

"Lions?" Denny demanded.

"You mean did I see them?" She didn't wait for him to confirm as she answered. "Yes. A group of us explored with local guides and saw quite a few animals in their natural habitat. You'd think that lions are the most terrifying, but they aren't. It's the crocodile. A gazelle goes innocently for a drink of water, and the crocodile appears out of nowhere, like lightning, and pulls it under. It's horrifying."

"It sounds like it," Lila said with a shudder.

Rita's gaze went distant, seeing something that no one else could. Her pause was long and dark before she spoke again. "Rather like the last few days, really. Humans are more crocodile than lion. Devious and dangerous and attacking out of nowhere." She shuddered, and Kate stepped forward, wrapping an arm around Rita's shoulders and murmuring to her.

They headed up the stairs while the rest of them stared after. Violet finally broke from the spell.

Ham also had news that had disturbed even him. She glanced at him, the question in her eyes, and he said, "I'll explain later."

Which translated into that Jack would hear immediately but Violet would have to wait.

"Why don't the rest of us dress for dinner?" Victor said, dashing Denny's hopes. "We'll meet down here with the dinner gong?"

Jack glanced at Ham and jerked his head towards the library.

"Hardly fair," Violet told them, but Jack reminded her, "Glass, my love."

"You'll tell me?"

"To my utter dismay"—he paused to place a kiss on her brow —"your insights are invaluable."

That, Violet thought, deserved gratitude. She kissed his cheek before running up the stairs. The moment she entered her room, she rang the bell for Beatrice and asked the maid to rid Violet of the dress she was wearing, put the black pearls up for a while, and start the bath.

While Beatrice worked, Violet lay down on the end of her bed and simply breathed in and out. It had been a terrible few days, Violet thought, redeemed only by finally learning what it felt like to be held in Jack's arms through the whole of a night. If anything, Violet had become completely and utterly certain that all roads in her life led to Jack. He was the other half of her heart and nothing would do for Violet but to spend the rest of her days with him.

VIOLET WENT SEARCHING for Jack as soon as she was sure she was glass-free. She left off much of her makeup again, only darkening her brows and lashes and applying a light layer of lipstick. She was so tired from the day she ached, and she wanted to go back to her bed with Jack nearby.

He was in the room he'd used before, directly next door to Victor. Violet found Jack in a suit, his tie still undone, as he put on his dress shoes. She walked into the room as he rose and tied his tie for him.

"There," she told him, letting her hand trail down his chest. "You're perfect now."

"Hardly that." His eyes were worried and his jaw and shoulders were tight. Whatever they'd learned wasn't good.

"Well?" Violet tangled their fingers together and laid her cheek against his chest. There was something to be said for wearing very little makeup and not having to worry about it smudging his crisp black suit.

"They found the shooter."

Violet gasped and looked up at him. "What? How? *Who?*"

"An ex-soldier who hasn't been able to find work since he returned home. He never met the person who hired him face-to-face, but he was referred to whomever is setting this up by the man in the club. He gave us a name for that fellow, but we're having trouble tracking him down."

She blinked and opened her mouth to say something but had simply nothing to say. She gaped instead.

"The shooter, it seems, was told to miss you and Rita."

Violet had felt she was gaping before, but now she was well and truly fish-mouthed. "I—I don't understand."

"It's madness," Jack growled, "that's why. The shooter was told that he was only to scare Miss Russell."

Violet closed her eyes and pressed her forehead against Jack. It seemed that every time they reached the new lows of mankind, they found humanity could sink lower. "They succeeded. Was Mrs. Russell's murder an accident then? Or perhaps they meant to kill her after all." Violet looked up at Jack. "Jack, anyone could be this madman. It could be any family member. Any of them. Anyone else. It could even be Miss Russell."

Jack nodded. "We're back at square one. I'm not sure what to do from here. We've hardly had time to think on it. If they only mean to terrorize, we'll never know when they're done. I would say that Miss Russell fleeing home and staying with strangers is exactly what they want. As long as she's with us, they know she's scared."

"Perhaps then they won't strike again while she's with us," Violet surmised. "But for as long as it takes to find the culprit, she'll have to look over her shoulder."

"We'll figure it out," Jack swore. "I don't care if they meant to scare her or not. They put you at risk twice over and I intend to see them pay."

She wrapped her arms around his waist to remind him she was well. Eventually the dinner gong rang, but neither of them moved. They lingered in each other's arms, finding refuge and solace simply by the reality of their heart beats, each precious breath, the scent of each other, their warmth. In the end, they moved only because they could hear Victor running up the steps for them.

Before he could tease them, they stepped into the hall and went to join the others.

CHAPTER 15

*O*n-poisoned cocktails were just what was needed after the last few days. Non-poisoned cocktails with champagne because fizzy always made things better. Violet's drink was a random concoction she wasn't sure Victor could duplicate. She'd asked for something strong, fruity, and sweet. Whatever he'd put together tasted heavily of champagne and citrus and made Violet want to pick an orange from a tree and eat it warm, with the sun shining on her face. She could picture it so clearly, she was almost there.

Except Rita—who Violet was coming to like more and more—was in the room. Violet could feel the difference in the air caused by the presence of someone new. When adding in the recent events, Denny's desire to dive into the suspects, and Jack's tense worry, the entire evening felt disjointed. This wasn't their normal way of spending an evening together. Tonight no one would turn on the wireless, no one would feel or succumb to the urge to dance, and when they went to bed, they'd all be chased into their dreams by dark thoughts.

Violet turned to Rita. Their gazes met, Violet's dark to the brilliant blue of Miss Russell. She'd bathed and washed her hair and put it into finger waves. The style suited Miss Russell immensely. She looked as if she'd stepped out of the moving pictures with her glorious good looks.

"It seems like anyone as beautiful as you would have someone who obsessed of her," Violet suggested.

At her statement, Denny leaned forward, eyes alight with joy. He set his cocktail down with a click and took in a deep breath, holding it to contain what might well have been a squeal of excitement.

"Why are you saying that?" Rita asked. The woman was sharp, Violet had to admit.

"We found the shooter," Hamilton Barnes said and then lit a cigarette. "He wasn't trying to kill you. He was trying to scare you."

"Why?" Rita demanded.

"That is the question of the hour, isn't it? If murder isn't the final goal, why are you being targeted?"

"I don't know," Rita wailed. "I have no idea."

Violet believed her. She needed another cocktail, she thought, even though she wasn't half finished with the one in her hand. She wanted her mind to go blurry and things to seem funny that weren't all that amusing. Instead, Violet set her drink aside.

"It has to be that I'm back, right?" Rita guessed. "That's all that's changed in my life. I have been traveling for years. My love affairs have ended easily enough. No one expected me to accept a marriage proposal. I've always made it clear that wasn't what I wanted."

"Maybe they thought they could change your mind," Victor suggested. "I would have tried to change Kate's mind for the rest of her life if she'd said no to me."

"That's why she said yes," Rita told him. "You *love* her. The only man who tried to change my mind didn't have the money to live the life he was living and he was chased by creditors. Even then, he didn't do me the disservice of pretending to love me. He simply promised to entertain me for the rest of my days."

"Oh honey," Lila said lazily, "he would have been cheating on you within a year."

"We were never exclusive to each other," Rita said disgustedly. "He already had a lover he liked quite a bit more than me. She was as poor as he was."

Kate rubbed her swollen belly and glanced at Violet. The three women in the room, outside of Rita, had the luxury of being certain they were adored. The only way to rile Denny at all was to upset Lila. Victor wasn't just in love, he was grateful to be loved, completely convinced that Kate was too good for him. He often said he'd stolen a wittier, more righteous man's fated love and had to guard against her falling in love with someone else. As though it would be inevitable if he wasn't careful. His devotion was something poets would write sonnets about if only they could measure the depth and width of his feelings.

What if someone felt that way about Rita and was trying to drive her to him? It was an insane way to go about it, but nothing in all this made sense.

"It's been a rather long while since I was even half in a relationship," Rita told the others, squashing Violet's brief idea. "Before Africa certainly. It's a blur of boredom in that realm for some time."

"Has anything else changed in your life?"

Rita shook her head. "Since my mother died, I have traveled extensively. Father came back to England. Aunt Albright tried fervently to convince me to go home with her before and after India, but I refused. She came back when I wouldn't return after India. I traveled with friends for a long time. Father and I would meet in funny little places for a few weeks before he'd go home to England and I'd go on another adventure."

"Where did you meet?" Violet took another small sip of her drink.

"Crete once. A little village in Portugal. The south of Spain. Eventually, I traveled with a paid companion as though it were 1814 and I weren't a modern woman. An experienced missionary's wife who had been widowed. It made Father feel better. My mother wasn't around to object, but I think she would have. She'd have told Father to find his inner-conqueror and go with me to where the wind blew us. She was the life of our lives. After her, Father and I were always a little dour together."

"How did you lose your mother?" Lila asked gently.

"She grew sick and died. It was so fast. She faded like someone snuffed out her light. I always felt like we needed her too much. She didn't have the energy to provide joy for all of us anymore."

Goodness, Violet thought, she couldn't do this right now. She rose and paced while the others watched.

"Don't mind, Vi," Denny told Rita almost kindly. "She can't sit still when she's thinking."

"What is she thinking about?" Rita asked in a low voice, as if she didn't want to interrupt.

"Either Jack—always the most likely answer," Denny teased, "or as far as I can tell, random little shreds of clues that no one else even noticed. I think she paces and they churn up in her head. Then suddenly the pieces all fall together and we mortals look on in awe."

Violet glanced his way and saw him pick up the box of chocolates he'd arranged and hold one out to Rita. "The square ones have caramel and almonds, and, I think, the breath of angels, because they are divine."

Violet didn't *have* clues. She had nothing. A poor girl who had come home from her travels to find her father married to another woman. A younger woman. Who—it seemed—he had actually loved. How strange it must have been to realize her father had married a woman so much younger than even herself. Would that be something to spur Rita to murder? Violet didn't want to think so because she liked Rita. If, however, Rita had wanted to murder her stepmother and come out innocent, then setting herself up as the intended victim was a very clever way to do it.

Violet paced her usual route while twisting the ring on her finger, her usual pacing habit. She walked behind the couches, over to the wall, turned right, and paced in front of the couches, between her friends and the hearth, before reaching the doorway and turning once again. Her brother would eventually have to replace the carpets because of her pacing.

"Your stepmother *was* flashy," Violet said randomly. "If you were to tell someone to murder the flashy blonde in the black dress and then stand the two of you together, she would be the flashy one. Were you with her the whole evening?"

"Except when I was dancing," Rita admitted.

"So, if the waiter was told to switch drinks for the flashy blonde and she was indicated, it could have been her as the intended victim the whole time. *Or*, it could have been you and the person assumed that the waiter knew. Which really doesn't make sense."

"It's impossible to know," Jack said. "I asked and asked again, and the waiter said that he was told the flashy blonde, and he assumed that Mrs. Russell was the intended person."

"If I were being crass and referring to Miss Russell," Lila mused lazily, "I'd have referred to her being too-brown, but perhaps that is a woman thing? Do you notice her color first, Denny?"

Denny considered, staring at Miss Russell until she blushed. She lifted a game brow and held out her hands as if to ask him to examine her. His head tilted and he admitted, "With her blonde hair and blue eyes, her tan is all the more noticeable. It's quite attractive really. I would know exactly who you meant if you said the tanned blonde. I think that would be a more accurate term than flashy."

Violet had stopped her pacing to watch them interact. "Jack?"

"I agree. I'd use tanned and blonde before I'd use flashy with Miss Russell. She *could* be flashy, but given the differences in their figures, the daring dress on Miss Russell was rather shocking on Mrs. Russell. With her diamond necklace hovering near her chest and the low lights reflecting it, flashy is quite the right term for Mrs. Russell. Still, however, blonde in the black dress was quite accurate a description for both Miss Russell and Mrs. Russell."

"Perhaps," Hamilton cut in, "the phrase would be accurate for both women. And perhaps, flashy would be the more accurate term for Mrs. Russell when comparing the two women. However," Hamilton added, "flashy is also a term that can be quite derogatory."

"It is really," Lila said. "I wouldn't be thrilled if someone used that term on me or someone I loved."

"Exactly my point," Hamilton agreed. "It suggests the feeling of the speaker towards the woman he intended. If you despised either Miss

Russell or Mrs. Russell, the term would work for the speaker. We have no way of knowing who the person giving the initial description actually felt. Flashy is almost beside the point."

"What is the point," Violet said rather suddenly, "is the feeling—like you said, Hamilton. Whoever the victim was intended to be, the feeling behind that poisoning was of pure and abiding hatred."

"It usually is with murder, isn't it?" Rita said.

The rest of them shook their heads.

"Sometimes it's love, as odd as that seems," Denny said. "People are a bit twisted in the head, Rita."

"Or it's greed," Lila added. "It's just the ease of the moment. They don't really care about the victim at all. Just the money."

"But hemlock though," Vi said, "that isn't the easiest way to poison someone, right? You can get cyanide rather easily for rats. Hemlock is harder, isn't it?"

"It is," Hamilton agreed. "I see what you mean. You wouldn't pursue it first when there are other easier ways to kill someone. Not unless you *wanted* them to suffer."

"You are too clever for your own good, Vi," Jack told her.

CHAPTER 16

*V*iolet stared at the chalkboard the next morning. She was by herself in the parlor since it was very early. She had, in fact, slipped out of the bed, leaving Jack still sleeping, dressed in the bath, and tiptoed from her room. He had been exhausted, but she had fallen asleep with him tracing her freckles again, and she wasn't all that convinced that he'd slept until far after she had. That realization that they'd almost lost each other, yet again, had haunted him into the night while she'd slept secure in the feel of his arms. For her, she needed to feel his warmth. For him, he needed to see her breathing.

Hargreaves had seen Violet coming down the stairs. "Lady Violet, I'm afraid we weren't prepared for anyone to be up quite so early in the breakfast room. Would you like me to hurry the kitchens along?"

She'd declined. "Would you bring me Turkish coffee in the parlor? Also, see if we have a second chalkboard."

And so Violet had come to stand in front of the chalkboard in the favored parlor where they spent their normal evenings. They hadn't used it the night before, given that Denny had the chalkboard ready, and Jack had made it clear they weren't sure of Miss Russell.

Violet had understood why, but did Miss Russell realize she was a suspect? Instead of pursuing suspects, Violet erased the board and wrote: PEOPLE INVOLVED

She then listed a series of names with space behind them. She was frowning as she wrote:

MR. RUSSELL—Rita's father.

MRS. MELODY RUSSELL—poisoning victim.

RITA RUSSELL—daughter, victim of shooting episode, possible intended victim of poisoning.

MRS. RUSSELL, the first—Rita's mother.

MRS. JEAN ALBRIGHT — Rita's aunt, the first Mrs. Russell's sister, Mr. Russell's sister-in law.

Violet considered for several minutes about who else had been included in the case. It was so obscure. Hamilton, Jack, and the other policemen were working the case and turning up information that Violet would never have found, like the shooter. She could only focus on those she had met or that she knew of. Her head tilted as she considered and then she added:

MAN WHO DELIVERED THE HEMLOCK—tall, thin, dark grey hair, wore a ring with a double infinity symbol.

MAN WHO SHOT THE GUN—was hired to just scare, not hurt, Rita. How did he know where she would be? How did he know what she looked like?

WAITER FROM THE CLUB —perhaps the poisoner was all a lie? Could the information he provided be trusted?

MR. RUSSELL'S ELDER BROTHER — if Rita were to die, he would be a possible heir.

MR. RUSSELL'S YOUNGER BROTHER — if Rita were to die, he would be a possible heir.

WOMEN FROM THE LADIES CLUB —would they have known that Rita was going to that club that evening? Would they have any reason to want Rita dead? What about Melody Russell? She had shown herself to be willing to play a little dirty when she'd threatened Violet. Could she have done the same to someone from the club?

Violet was pacing in front of the board when Hargreaves returned with two footmen and a second board. "I wasn't sure you'd find another."

A kitchen maid entered the room next with a tray with the coffee cup, sweet rolls, and a bowl of fruit. Violet grinned at her favorite things and then thanked them as they left her again. She poured herself coffee as she stared at the second board, and then she started a timeline on the it.

1— The first Mrs. Russell died.

2— Mrs. Albright joins Rita in India traveling for ___.

3— Mr. Russell returns home to England

4— Rita travels the world, eventually going to Africa and then coming home

4a—Sometime during Rita's Africa (?) trip Mr. Russell meets and marries Melody Russell.

Nothing they'd learned seemed to connect to the events she'd written down so far, but the events were the earliest that Violet knew. She stretched out her neck and sipped her coffee as she lifted the chalk once again. As she did, the door opened and Denny demanded, "How can you do this without me?"

Violet glanced over her shoulder. "I couldn't sleep for thinking of it. There's a magic in writing things down. You see things that weren't there before."

He frowned at her and then spoke over his shoulder into the hall, "Send in more coffee and tea, please, Hargreaves. I saw Jack shaving and prettying up."

Violet ignored Denny as she wrote:

5—Rita Russell returns to England. (She's enjoying her time here. How long has she been back?)

"That does matter, doesn't it?" Denny agreed. "Perhaps there were little disturbing things happening to Mrs. Russell before we were on the scene, and we had no idea. Shall I make a list of questions?"

"That's a good idea," Violet told him and had Denny join her at the chalkboard. She glanced his way and grinned at him.

His golden blonde hair was slicked back, and his blue eyes glinted with a rare interest. He was, she noticed, on a bit of a downturn in his weight. He went up and down in his size directly associated to whether his wife, Lila, was compelling him to exercise.

"How much trouble am I in for that last box of chocolates?"

Denny's smirk told her that Lila hadn't been pleased. The two of them were, without question, the biggest chocolate addicts among their friends.

"Not as much as I would have been should I have brought them home," Denny replied. "She's always so sweet about it. Denny love," he said in a high-pitched tone, "I need you to live a long life or at least last until I die first."

Violet laughed as Denny wrote out the questions: When did Rita return to England? and Did anything happen to Mrs. Russell before she returned?

"You know what would be convenient," Denny muttered, "one of those journals you women keep. It could say something like Dear Diary, so-and-so threatened me today and I fear for my life. Then you or Jack could just trap them with your questions, and we could all go out dancing again without fearing for our lives."

Violet was laughing as Lila and Jack appeared in the doorway.

"They look cozy, don't they?" Lila asked Jack.

"That's not love, your husband hitting Violet," Jack told Lila, "that's her first cup of her Turkish coffee."

Violet lifted her cup to Jack and Lila, who both smirked back.

"Oh I'm not jealous of these two," Lila announced, "they're the same as grubby siblings."

"Dear beloved," Denny said, as he poured Lila a cup of tea and handed it to her, "I would never dare to step out on you. You would certainly slay me, and Violet loves you more than me, so she wouldn't even catch you and make you pay."

"Too right, laddie," Lila told him, but her eyes were smiling, and the two of them were as certain of the other as Violet and Jack were.

"That is the question, isn't it though?" Jack said, taking in the chalkboards as Hamilton entered the room. "What about Mrs.

Russell? Just because her husband seems to have loved her doesn't mean he didn't find out she was straying. Being played the cuckold is a murder incentive for many a man."

"There isn't any evidence yet," Hamilton said, "of such a thing. It's on the list of questions that the boys are looking into. I've got Petey working the case too. Mr. Russell is too wealthy and too well connected to not have as many boys as possible working this thing. We need it wrapped up and quick."

"Is Father harassing you?" Rita asked, as she also entered the parlor. She paused as she saw the two chalkboards. She froze as she read them. "Is this how you do it? You write it all out and discuss?"

Lila shrugged and sipped her tea, entirely uncaring of the way Rita's life being laid out might affect her. Denny nodded happily and told her, "It is rather fun, you'll see." His head tilted and he grinned engagingly at her. "Unless, of course, you killed Mrs. Russell."

"I?"

"Don't be stupid," Denny told Rita with that same charming, boyish grin. "You have to know you're on the list of suspects."

"But why would I?"

"Your father married a child, and she was driving you mad," Denny explained. "If this were a book, you'd be my number one suspect until we found out that Mrs. Russell was stepping out on your father. Then, we'd discover it was him. Why would anyone just try to *scare* you?"

Rita answered for them, so they didn't have to. "Because I was trying to make it seem it wasn't me, or they love me."

"Exactly," Denny told her happily. "Isn't this fun?"

"Mmm," she answered, her expression a very sound no.

"This is what you asked for," Lila told Rita, unsympathetically. "Finding a killer isn't a very kind business."

"It hurts when it's you or the people you love."

"We know that," Lila said with that same lack of sympathy. "Denny's brother was on that board not too long ago. Violet's whole family has passed over that board."

Rita's brows lifted. She accepted a cup of tea from Violet, and they all turned to the boards.

"I want to know who benefits from Melody dying," Rita said. "I refuse to believe my father killed her. You can put him on your list, but I reject that idea."

"Of course you do," Hamilton told her. His gaze lingered on Rita's face, and Violet's eyes widened. She shot her gaze at Jack, who saw the same interest on their friend's face. They turned as one to Ham. He saw their question and shot them both a look that was a clear command to leave him alone.

Rita Russell was beautiful beyond most women. With her blonde hair, blue eyes, and even features, she was near perfection in a feminine form. Add in the daring and she had to be almost intoxicating, Violet thought, to the discerning man.

She winked at Ham.

"So Rita, tell us," she asked, "who loves you?"

"I thought we'd already discussed that my lovers moved on without much regret."

Violet's lips twitched when Ham bit back an objection, but she simply said, "I don't mean lovers only. I mean anyone who has or does ever love you. Denny, a list! Write Mr. Russell and Mrs. Russell the first. Who else?"

Rita's mouth twisted and she took in a deep breath. "What a terrible thing to discover you aren't sure who else you can add to such a list. People who love Rita? Her parents—" Her gaze moved around the room, never quite meeting anyone's eyes. She sighed. "Well and truly loves me? Aunt Jean. Mrs. Greene, the missionary who travels with me. Ah, perhaps my uncle Eddie is somewhat fond of me. Uncle Malcolm does not appreciate independent women, let alone more adventurous women like myself. He never really liked my mother, either."

Denny added the three names. Violet stared at them and considered who would go on her list. There would be far more names, Violet knew. She turned to Rita. "Just because you travel doesn't mean you can't build relationships, Rita. It's time to make friends."

Rita nodded and sipped her tea, but what could she say?

Violet was a busybody on occasion, but she refrained from the insulting comment that you started by being a friend. If she'd moved and followed her adventurous mother her whole life, continuing on alone, then she may have never learned how to make those early forays into long-term friendship.

CHAPTER 17

*T*hey left for breakfast as a group while Victor and Kate loaded into Victor's automobile. Victor had determined to motor down to the country houses so they could stop whenever Kate needed. She was sending him loving glances as Victor consulted with Jack on the locations where Kate might stretch her legs or use the ladies.

Violet grinned at her brother while she was sitting on a table in the great hall, swinging her legs.

"Is this," Denny demanded, "what comes of procreating? Where is that lad I once knew? The one who took the train so he could squeeze in a few extra cocktails for his long weekend."

"It is, indeed," Victor told Denny merrily. "I'm off to buy a house with the right kind of nursery and garden, my lad. The days of freedom and booze are gone, and we're onto nappies and I don't know. What else do babies do?"

"Cry," Lila told him. "Endlessly."

"Poo," Denny added. "Spit up."

"Love Auntie Vi and despise dear, old dad."

Victor scowled at all of them and announced, "You're next."

"Too right," Ham said. "Would you mind dropping me on your way?" He glanced at Jack and added, "I'll be back."

Violet handed Kate a basket. "You're visiting Ginny, yes?"

Kate nodded.

"These are for her."

Victor, Kate, and Ham left and the rest of them glanced at each other. Violet had stepped into the kitchens earlier to get sweets for Ginny and had seen that there were two constables in the kitchens having breakfast. They blushed and rose when Violet saw them, but she simply waved them back and told them to enjoy. There was another watching the street, she knew, and they were changing in and out.

Would Jack end up leaving to work as well, or was he going to stay? When she looked at him, he gestured with a tilt of his chin towards the parlor. Ah, she thought, time to question Rita more. They brought her back to the room. Violet examined the chalkboards. Rita rose and stood next to Violet and then she asked for the chalk.

Vi handed it over and stepped back next to Denny, who rubbed his hands together and then zipped his mouth. They grinned at each other while Rita looked at the timeline. Before she lifted the eraser, it read:

1— The first Mrs. Russell died.

2— Mrs. Albright joins Rita in India traveling for ___.

3— Mr. Russell returns home to England

4— Rita travels the world, eventually going to Africa and then coming home

4a—Sometime during Rita's Africa (?) trip Mr. Russell meets and marries Melody Russell

5—Rita Russell returns to England. (She's enjoying her time here. How long has she been back?)

Violet and the rest watched as Rita began writing.

1—Harriet and Philip marry.

2—Rita is born.

3—Philip takes a job with Bank of Mountmarch.

4—Philip, Harriet, and Rita move to Russia.

5—Philip, Harriet, and Rita move to Spain.*
Somewhere in here, Melody is born.
6—Philip, Harriet, and Rita move to Greece.
7—Jean Albright is widowed and moves to Greece.
8—Philip, Harriet, Rita, and Jean move to—

"Why are you adding all the extra bits?" Denny demanded.

"It makes me feel better to include Mother, even if she doesn't matter to the investigation—she matters to me."

"Ignore him and proceed," Jack directed, shooting Denny a quiet-down order with just a look.

Rita finished:

—India.

9—Harriet Russell dies.
10—Philip Russell takes a home office position.
11—Jean and Rita tour India.
12—Jean and Rita go to Spain for a ramble.
13—Jean returns to England.
14—Rita travels to Africa with Mrs. Greene.
15—Phillip marries Melody.
15a—Rita returns to England.

She told the others, "I came home, met Melody, and fled. I went to Paris for six days and then decided I needed to be the modern woman I wanted to be and face my life. I came home, looked up old friends, and pretended I wasn't bothered by having a stepmother a decade younger than myself. A good friend of mine from India was a member of the Piccadilly Ladies Club and she invited me. That became my refuge, and I was making my own friends, discovering clubs, being accepted by women who found my travels exciting rather than odd."

"Only Melody dug further and further into your life." Violet refilled her coffee cup, realized she was feeling the most refreshed she had in simply ages, and left the refilled coffee on the table. "Until she turned her gaze on the club."

Rita continued writing on the board:

16—Met Emily Allen and heard a tirade on Violet Carlyle after someone suggested that Lady Violet would be an excellent addition to the ladies club.

17—Met Lady Isolde on a walk and later had tea with her, hearing more about Lady Violet and discovering where she shopped.

18—Lied to Melody about joining the Piccadilly Ladies Club.

19—Tracked down Lady Violet and persuaded her to tea.

20—Lady Violet picked up the gauntlet of excluding Melody from the club.

21—Cocktails and jazz at the Sakura Club, Melody is poisoned and soon dies.

22—Asked Lady Violet for help with Melody's impending death.

23—Shots fired.

Violet paced while Rita returned to the tea tray and poured herself a cup. "It's rather horrible to see it laid out like that. To somehow turn the transition of Melody from a vibrant, frivolous woman into chalk and words on a board."

"She's far more than that," Jack told Rita. He stood and crossed to where Violet was pacing, standing just a few steps in front of her route., but when he spoke, it was to Rita again. "Do you know if anything was happening before you came back? Anything that caused alarm for your father or Melody?"

"I haven't been very close to Father since we separated in India. I still love him, of course, and hc me. Mother was the bridge between us. She would tell me what Father thought, and I imagine she would tell him the things I said to her."

"Did your Aunt Jean try to fill that role?" Violet asked. "There was overlap between when your mother was living and when you traveled without her. Did she contribute after? She must have known that your mother bridged you and your father."

"She did. She'd write him long, chatty letters after we separated and tell him everything about what we were doing. After I went onto my separate trips, she'd write me long, chatty letters about Father, family gatherings, my cousins, things that were happening in London. Gossip about people in her life."

Violet took the chalk up and wrote between 13 & 14—Jean takes up the role of bridging Rita and her father.

"Tell me more about your mother," Violet said. She felt as though she didn't have a handle on the family at all. They seemed entirely foreign to her.

Rita nodded and started to explain. "Mama was perfection. Beautiful, charming, she was utterly different from Melo—oh, Father."

Mr. Russell walked into the room, causing everyone to look up a bit guiltily. Mr. Russell looked as though he'd caved in on himself. His clothes were perfectly put together because, certainly, he had servants to look after him. Even still, his shoulders curved in. He had dark circles under his eyes.

He glanced at the chalkboard and then demanded, "I thought you were finding my wife's killer, not gossiping with my daughter." He was speaking directly Jack. "Get about it already."

"Father," Rita said softly, and he turned on her with an enraged gaze.

"Your mother is gone. She died and left us, and we had to carry on. I won't feel guilty for finding something else, something different with Melody."

"Father, that—"

He looked at his daughter so fiercely that Violet felt the need to interfere and took a breath, but Jack shook his head. He was watching the two of them avidly.

"Enough, Rita!"

"No," she snapped back. "We're suspects in this. They think that we could have had a reason to kill Melody. You could have. The cuckolded older man who married a woman too young and too pretty. We're going to answer their questions so we can get on with our lives. If Melody loved you, she wouldn't want her murder to go unsolved, nor would she want you blamed for it!"

"Blamed? Murdered?" Mr. Russell slumped into a seat, all the fight escaping him.

Gently, Rita said, "Answer their questions Father. They're good people. They're not going to do anything other than use the information to try to find a killer."

"I—don't see how the differences between Melody and my Harriet matter to this," Mr. Russell said.

Violet's head tilted at the differences there. Melody. Just Melody. And *my* Harriet. Violet was the one who answered because she thought that he might accept the answer a little easier from her.

"I can't explain why," Violet told him, pouring him a cup of tea and gesturing to Denny to get something stiffer from the bar in the corner. Denny returned a moment later, and Violet added more whiskey than tea. "It's just the full picture helps us pick out the frayed edges. It's easier to understand."

"That's all?"

Violet nodded and promised, "That's all. We just need a picture to start with."

He frowned and rubbed at his chest. "Harriet was perfection. Rita had it right. My first wife wasn't just beautiful—and she was. You've seen my daughter. You've even met Jean, who looks similar enough to Harriet—paler, less vibrant version of Harriet that Jean is. That can give you an idea." He sipped the tea, then set it down and continued.

"She was ambitious for both of us. She pushed for those well-paying, difficult positions in the far reaches of the world. She did it because she wanted to see the world. War or no war. My wife knew what she wanted, and she pulled Rita and me along with her. Rita grew up to be as she is. She would never have been anything different after such a life with her mother. Jean tried so hard to get Rita to come home, to consider college, to use her position to meet and marry someone like your group here, but Rita wouldn't have it."

"I thought Jean traveled with Rita?" Violet wondered.

"She did, but she had no passion for it. When Harriet died in India, Jean wanted us all to go home. I finished my assignment. Jean had joined us when her husband died, leaving her with nothing."

"How does she live?" Violet asked, frowning. She wouldn't have thought that the put-together woman she'd met would have been a poor relation.

"My wife included Jean in her will. Not a huge amount, but enough to allow Jean to be comfortable. They had money in their own right. Both of them. My wife and I used hers as seed money to grow a fortune with what I knew of banking and investments. Jean's husband frittered hers away and died poor and bankrupt."

What did the once poor sister matter? "Did you have any indication that Melody might have another person in her life?" Violet asked.

Mr. Russell blinked at the switch rather stupidly and flushed. "I know you won't believe me, but we loved each other, she and I. She wasn't seeing another man."

"Was she acting oddly at all?"

Mr. Russell frowned and admitted, "She had been since Rita came home. Jean was around more, and between the two of them, Melody stopped feeling like she was enough. Jean had been critical of Harriet. She was worse, far worse, when it came to Melody. I had to tell Jean that she had to respect Melody as my wife or return to her own family. It wasn't very kind of me, I'm afraid."

CHAPTER 18

*V*iolet was back to pacing as Jack thoroughly questioned Mr. Russell about his business. He had left his position at the bank even though he'd become a partner in it and owned a large portion. There wasn't any bad blood between him and his partners. His brothers had no expectations of more than simple bequests. Rita was his only heir now that Melody had died, and the bulk of the funds had never been changed from Rita.

"Her life won't change," Mr. Russell said, giving his daughter a bit of a worried expression. "She had no reason to kill Melody. I've always given her a large allowance. She could do anything she wanted with the money she has access to now."

"Did you ask her to stay? To stop traveling?"

Both of them said no. Violet's mouth twisted, and she spun the ring on her finger. Her fingers itched, and she felt certain she was missing the most important part of this madness.

"If Rita dies," Violet started, "your brothers?"

"I told them I was changing my will. It never benefited them before, but I assumed Rita would outlive me and didn't have any other plans. Now, the money will go into a trust that will see to the education of my nieces and nephews and then needy children. No one will materially benefit by Rita's death. My own death puts the money in Rita's care. I fear she'll be the judge then. They know she has little reason to leave anything to them or her cousins."

"What about the other side of the family?"

Mr. Russell shook his head. "There's only Rita and Jean."

"Maybe there is someone else," Violet started. She was going to say that perhaps Mrs. Russell would have had a lover, and Violet could see that, but it didn't explain Rita's near-miss where the shooter had been told to not hurt Rita.

"Nothing adds up," Violet said. "Nothing but Rita or Mr. Russell."

"We didn't," Rita argued. "Father would never, and I don't have any reason to."

"I agree with you there," Violet said, pouring herself a tea and whiskey. "If you had reason to kill Melody, it would be because she was having a baby or something, but the doctor told Jack she wasn't expecting."

"She was young," Mr. Russell said. "She asked me if I minded if we didn't have children right away, and I told her that we'd do whatever she wished. Even then, I would have seen to that child certainly, but the money I have now—it came because of Harriet. I could never take it from Harriet's only child and give it to another, and my will attests to that. The money I set aside for Melody would have been given to any children we had. It's there in black and white. The bulk of the money would have gone to Rita. My other children would be well enough off, but it wasn't an even split. Not even close."

Violet wanted to slam her hand down on the table and demand the truth, but anything that Mr. Russell said would be verified. Jack, Ham, whoever else was assigned to this case would ensure that what he said was the truth. Mr. Russell couldn't be so stupid that he didn't know that. If he was lying, it wasn't about something they would catch him in.

Violet left the parlor after she finished her tea and ran up the stairs to her bedroom. She didn't have anything she needed to do; she was just frustrated that they had nothing. She paced the hall while Jack asked questions that would lead them nowhere. Either Mr. Russell knew exactly why Melody had been killed or it had been a random act.

But no. Violet would have almost bought a random act but for the shooting at the ladies club. Whoever was behind Melody's death had ruined a very clever murder by being cheeky. Violet's head tilted and she ran down the stairs. She walked into the parlor and spun the chalkboards around for the cleaned back.

On the first she wrote: MELODY RUSSELL. On the second, Violet wrote: RITA RUSSELL.

Under each of the names she wrote motives for murder.

GREED-

LOVE-

JEALOUSY-

HATRED-

MERCY-

SELF DEFENSE-

ANGER -

POWER-

Violet considered her notes for a few minutes and then on Mrs. Russell's board, Violet wrote behind MERCY — There was nothing merciful about this death. Hemlock poisoning is painful. Did anyone have a reason to hate her? Violet then crossed out Mercy.

Under ANGER—she wrote, The death was clearly fore-planned. This was no act of fury in the moment to be regretted over afterward. She then crossed out anger.

"So you're going from another angle?" Denny stood next to Violet and started working Rita's board. He crossed out mercy and anger and self-defense. Violet didn't object to those choices, so she left him to it and considered greed. She wrote: Melody left no money to anyone. There was no clear financial benefit. No one was affected financially by her death.

She turned to Rita and Mr. Russell and asked, "Would you say this is correct?"

Neither objected, so Violet crossed out greed. She glanced at the rest of the motives, considering each of them separately while Rita joined Denny and helped him work on her board.

Violet moved to the next obviously wrong motive and crossed out self-defense. Under hatred she wrote: Someone hated her terribly to choose hemlock over all other poisons. What did Melody do that caused so much anger? Violet considered for a long time and then wrote: She married Mr. Russell.

Violet was working quickly then, and when she finished, she stepped away and looked over the board:

GREED- Melody left no money to anyone. There was no clear financial benefit. No one was affected financially by her death.

LOVE- The person who loved Mrs. Russell was Mr. Russell. Could she have had another lover? A question for the yard men to pursue.

JEALOUSY- Mr. Russell's love? Attention?

HATRED- Someone hated her terribly to choose hemlock over all other poisons. What did Melody do that caused so much anger? She married Mr. Russell.

MERCY- There was nothing merciful about this death. Hemlock poisoning is painful. Did anyone have a reason to hate her?

SELF-DEFENSE

ANGER - the death was clearly fore-planned. This was no act of fury in the moment to be regretted over afterward.

POWER-

She turned to speak to Mr. Russell, but she saw that Denny and Rita had finished their own board. They switched places and read each other's notes.

GREED- Perhaps. Rita is very wealthy. If she died, *someone* would benefit.

LOVE- No current lovers. Her father didn't benefit from her death. Why would Jean target Rita? Is the only reason she survived because she was loved? But anyone who loved her would have no reason to scare her.

JEALOUSY- Rita's life is too empty to be jealous of.

HATRED- Why would they leave her alive if they hated her? No.

MERCY-

SELF DEFENSE

ANGER -

POWER -

Violet spun the board around that listed the people that loved Rita. They were:

Mrs. Russell.

Mr. Russell.

Jean Albright.

Mrs. Greene.

Uncle Eddie.

"Oh," Violet said, staring in horror. "Oh. Oh, no."

Violet spun to the others and Denny clapped his hands, tossed a guilty look to the Russells and declared, "She figured something out."

"What is it?"

"It's here," Violet said. "It's right here before us. Tell me about your double infinity rings."

Mr. Russell frowned. "Are you referring to the rings the boys and I wore in school?"

"I don't know," Violet said. "You had a double infinity ring?"

"I did. I—I was on a rowing team. All the boys had them. I wore it for a while after. We all did, I'd guess, for as long as that part of our lives was important. When we got them, it seemed like it would be forever. Five years later I had set it aside, and I don't think I ever put it back on."

"What happened to your ring?"

"I have no idea," Mr. Russell said, staring at Violet as if she were mad. "What does it matter? It's been years since I had it. Rita used to play with it, I think. Yes," he nodded. "Her mother put a few pieces of unused jewelry in a box for Rita when she was small. It was her jewelry box so Rita would leave Harriet's things alone. I haven't seen it since then."

"I remember that," Rita said. "I loved that box. I added my own things later, when I got older. Mama got me that cameo broach. I was so excited when I added it. There was the charm bracelet. Eventually, my first strand of pearls. I still have the jewelry box. But—I haven't seen that ring in ages. Not since India, I guess. Maybe after? No." She shook her head. "No. It wasn't in the box when I gathered my things after the Spain ramble."

Violet nibbled her bottom lip and spun Melody Russell's board to the list of people involved. "Who on this list would have known about that ring?"

"My brothers, I suppose."

"Aunt Jean would have known," Rita added. "She used to go through the box with me. She taught me how to polish it all."

"And she was there when Mrs. Harriet Russell died."

Violet erased Melody's board and added Harriet Russell with the motives:

GREED- Jean Albright went from a poor relation to having money.

LOVE- Jean Albright lived in the house with the successful, handsome, devoted Mr. Russell. How attractive that must have been.

JEALOUSY- Jean had the same start as Harriet, yet look at the differences.

HATRED- Would jealousy turn a sister's love to hatred? Were they devoted at all? Perhaps they were simple strangers.

MERCY-

SELF DEFENSE

ANGER - Very possibly.

POWER- Jean went from poor relation to the adviser of Rita, the bridge between Rita and Philip. She went from almost useless to needed—at least for a while.

"No," Rita gasped. "Oh my goodness, no. Not Mama. No."

"Did Mrs. Albright know you were going on a date?"

Rita nodded and then furiously hissed, "She knew that Melody wanted to join us as well."

"Who beyond Mr. Russell and Mrs. Albright knew you'd be at the club?"

Rita shook her head over and over again before Jack said, "Miss Russell, answer the question."

"Only Aunt Jean knew. I complained to her so often about Melody. I'm sorry Papa. I didn't realize."

"She made overtures," Mr. Russell said, sounding exhausted, "after my wife died and before I returned to England. She suggested we could be a family still, without Harriet. I told her I'd never entertain the idea."

Rita bit down on her lip as she wiped a sudden tear away. "She told me that our family would never be complete if I kept flitting about the world without Papa. She said Papa needed us to come home. When I told her I couldn't face it without Mama, she told me I was a selfish child, and she'd ensure Father was well without me."

"You're her pseudo-daughter," Violet said. "She wanted you afraid, but not hurt. As long as you survive, she could use you to get to Mr. Russell."

"Violet," Jack said. "I cannot strangle a woman."

"Of course you can," Violet told him, trying and failing for merry. "Men have been strangling women for ages."

"You may not be able to"—Mr. Russell stood, shoulders straight and eyes roiling with too many emotions to read—"but I will. If your fiancé is correct, and I know she is in my very soul, this woman murdered both of the women I loved. My…" Mr. Russell fell to his knees as he moaned. "My *Harriet.* She was my everything. I—"

He folded in on himself and the others left him to his daughter and his tears.

CHAPTER 19

"Now to trap her," Jack said.

"I say we just poison her as well and leave her to die alone. Possibly on a moor. Definitely in the cold," Lila suggested as she opened the door to the library. "I also recognize that we barely had breakfast, but I need a cocktail."

"You're a vengeful woman," Denny told his wife, snaking his arm around her waist and pulling her to him. "I love it. I'm going to need you to avoid your crazy sister all the more now." Lila smiled at him, and he dipped her back as if they were dancing and kissed her fiercely. When he looked up from his kiss, Denny told Violet, "Masterfully wicked thinking, my friend."

"How *are* we going to trap her?" Violet asked, as Denny made them all cocktails. He'd found the chocolate liqueur and sent a maid for cream. Denny only made one drink outside of a G&T, and it was chocolate liqueur, strawberry liqueur, white rum, cream, and ice. He always used a heavy hand on the chocolate liqueur, and the two of them had become sick on them more than once.

There was a knock on the door and Hargreaves stepped in. "There's luncheon prepared, my lady, if you'd like."

Denny poured himself the last of the mixed cocktail before leading the way to the dining room with a cocktail in each hand, while Violet and Jack went to invite the Russells.

They all came though the Russells looked sick. Violet took one look at them and told Hargreaves, "Perhaps the Russells would like some ginger wine. I find it to be most comforting when things are falling to pieces."

"They don't know that about you at the ladies club," Rita joked.

"Oh!" Violet said, "The ladies club—" Violet stared at her drink. "It's such an innocuous place. A perfect place for asking your aunt to meet you and telling her that the police suspect your father."

Rita stared at Violet, sipped her ginger wine, then set down her wineglass with shaking hands. "You want me to help you trap her?"

Violet nodded. "Send her a note. Tell her you stormed from here when you realized they were going to arrest Mr. Russell. Tell her you can discuss it further and need her help in saving your father."

Rita's hands didn't stop shaking, but she nodded. Violet glanced at Hargreaves, who left and returned with a pen and paper. Rita's hand was trembling as she wrote, and Violet saw more than one tear fall onto the page. She didn't say a word about the tears as they lent credence to the trap.

Rita finished and then cried into her soup. Her father didn't notice. He was too lost in his own thoughts. They were dark and terrible things by the expression on his face. When they finished with their meal, Jack told Mr. Russell they needed him at Scotland Yard. They left while Rita contacted the ladies club and spoke with one of the women who managed the place.

In the morning, they'd do their best to manipulate a murderess into confessing that she killed her own sister and a young woman both for having the sheer gall to marry the man Jean wanted. Violet sent Rita to her room when she didn't stop crying and sent Beatrice after with a sleeping draught to see her through the night.

"The part where the people around them realize why the person they loved was killed is not my favorite part," Denny said. "I'm glum now. Feels callous to send her off to bed and turn on some jazz music."

"I'd suggest we go shopping or out for a distraction," Lila said lazily, as she propped up her feet on the ottoman in front of her, "but I don't want Jack to murder me after he finishes with that Jean woman. What a terrible monster she is." Lila yawned delicately. "Does an afternoon and evening of lingering over cocktails seem as callous as dancing?"

"What if we curled up with a book," Violet suggested, already knowing she was going to spend the afternoon working on her own book. When Denny gave her the oddest look, she left him with Lila in the parlor and retreated to write.

Violet sat down to her desk. The stepmother in her story was both a combination of Lady Eleanor and Melody Russell, but that seemed too callous. Somehow the girl who had started as something of a blank slate became the girl who had fallen for a man old enough to be her father.

Her motives, however, adjusted as Violet recognized that whether Melody had loved Mr. Russell or not, Melody Russell *had been* loved. It was tragic the way her husband referred to his wives, though. Would she have died a little knowing that Harriet was 'my Harriet,' or had Melody known and accepted that her husband was still in love with his first wife?

Violet considered what she'd seen of him that day. He'd seemed well and truly upset when he'd appeared at the door to check on his daughter. She had thought he loved his young wife when all the fight left him. Yet when he'd learned that his Harriet hadn't fallen ill and died—that she'd been murdered—well, that had destroyed him. It had sent him to his knees, curled in on himself.

Violet started writing, the story telling itself, perhaps even exorcising itself. She didn't stop when the dinner gong rang because she didn't hear it. She wrote until Beatrice appeared with a tray of sandwiches and then carried on, long after forgetting to eat until Jack returned, picked up the chair she was sitting in and physically moved her away from her typewriter.

"Aren't you out of ink on your ribbon?"

Violet rubbed her eyes and yawned.

"Enough writing, Vi. We tracked down Russell's rowing team, as many as we could in a reasonable time. They confirmed the story of the double infinity ring. We tracked down those who knew Mrs. Albright. She was cagey, but her previous landlady said she talked about Mr. Russell rather a 'concerning amount.' During all of that, did you write?"

Vi nodded and admitted, "I turned the murder into part of the book. Not all of it, of course, but enough to make me feel better."

Jack leaned down and kissed her forehead. It was a short journey to her cheek and then her chin, and soon she found herself lifted and carried. He sat down on one of the large chairs near the fire with her kneeling over him, and it was easy for time to pass too quickly.

She pulled back when she couldn't breathe and met his gaze. It was nearly as hot as she was. She jerked in a breath when Denny spoke from the doorway.

"That might be a record. Remember those days, love? Before we gave up on being pure and good?"

Violet would have blushed, but as she was already so hot and flushed from Jack's kisses, her body couldn't turn any redder without combusting. Instead, she pressed her cheek to his chest and watched Denny and Lila in their casual leaning.

"Indeed, I do, my lad," Lila said. "These are more righteous souls than ours."

Denny's grin was so broad, Violet thought he might hurt himself. "I don't like you very much right now," Violet told him.

"Jack was the one who left the door open," Denny said and sniffed innocently. "This is hardly our fault if we were going for a bit of a stroll down the hall and discover something of a show on the other side of an *open* door."

"Victor bribed Denny to keep you from each other," Lila told them casually. "There's nothing doing but to give in and remain chaste on Denny's watch. He'll be far worse, you know, than Victor should Denny discover things progressing. There's a whole case of chocolate liqueur on the line from that little bottler near Paris who doesn't have any more for Denny to buy."

MURDER AT THE LADIES CLUB

"No matter the price," Denny squeaked. "Not for a while yet. I can't wait that long!"

"I like that liqueur," Violet declared, gaze narrowing.

"Earn it with me," Denny suggested. "I'll give you two bottles."

"Out of twelve? I'll give you two bottles."

"Are you bargaining with Denny about—"

Jack trailed off and Violet pulled away from his chest and grinned at him. "Maybe."

"Hmm," was Jack's only reply.

Violet stood, stretched out the kinks of writing, and then turned on Denny. "We aren't going to do anything. Go away."

"I know that," Denny told her. "You'd have been on the bed if Jack planned to do more than kiss you senseless. It was simply fun to harass you."

"He waited until he felt enough time had passed," Lila announced. "He tiptoed down the hall and waved me forward as if we were invading France."

Violet frowned fiercely but Denny giggled, picked up Lila, putting her over his shoulder, and left. He called back, "The door will be open on our side as well. Random inspections! Don't get comfortable."

"We could lock him out," Jack suggested. "But first, we have to go down to the cellar, get all the chocolate liqueur and move it to our house."

"There are so many reasons to love you," Violet told him, "but that is definitely high on the list. Ooh! Some of the strawberry liqueur too. Ooh, and both kinds of rum. Anything that looks fun."

"We could empty the whole cellar. Just to see the look on his face."

Violet laughed so hard it hurt. "I don't think you realize the level of that undertaking, and Victor might cry."

CHAPTER 20

*T*he ladies club was ready for them. They were open at all hours, but if you weren't a member, their doors didn't open until 9:00 a.m. even if you were meeting with someone there. Violet and Rita arrived at 7:30 a.m. with Jack in tow. Special circumstances had the ladies club making allowances. Hamilton Barnes was already there with Mr. Russell, who had been 'taken in' the previous evening. It had translated to Mr. Russell calling his solicitor and spending the evening at Ham's home. Violet noticed Ham's new pin-striped suit, which drew attention, she suddenly realized, to his much slimmer figure. How long had he been losing weight? Perhaps his old suit had hid the changes he'd been making?

Perhaps the suit meant nothing as Ham only went about his business, ordering events. To cover their bases, there were two constables across the street watching the ladies club and two men in the kitchens near the back doors.

Violet, Rita, and Mrs. Albright were going to be using a small private dining room that had a butler's pantry between the dining room and the hallway. Mr. Russell, Jack, and Ham would be in there, ready to step in should the circumstances require it. The staffed ensured that the food was ready and on the table so there would be no reason to open the butler's pantry door.

Mrs. Albright was late enough that Violet and Rita were pacing when the ladies club butler opened the door to the dining room. "Here you are, Mrs. Albright. So nice to see you again."

"Aunt Jean!" Rita said, tears coming to her gaze immediately. "Oh, Aunt Jean! Thank you for coming. I have been lost."

Jean rushed to Rita and wrapped her arms around the woman. Violet could see that Rita was stiff in her aunt's arms, but she made up for it with releasing fervent sobbing. "There, there," Jean said, rubbing Rita's back. "There, there, darling. Tell me all about it."

"It's the shooter. They caught him almost immediately," Rita sobbed. "He clued in the constables that things were off with this case. They think that Melody was stepping out on Father and that he murdered her and then hired someone to shoot at me. The man had orders just to scare me and make it seem like murder. As soon as they understood that I wasn't intended to be hurt, they said it would be someone who loved me."

"That makes no sense!" Jean snarled. "Why would someone who loved you pay that—that—*idiot* to shoot at you?"

"To hide their own crimes," Rita said, pulling away and looking at her aunt, searching her face. The dark circles under Rita's eyes and the tears that had to be clouding her vision did nothing to hide the brilliant blue of her gaze.

The aunt turned on Violet. "You believe this? You believe that her father would do such a thing?"

Violet made a commiserating face and gently, almost apologetically said, "They were able to track something on the man who arranged for the poison at the club. The waiter will be able to testify and it will link Philip to the poison. That's such a damning piece of evidence."

"But, but, but, the ring? Malcom has one of those rings as well. That double infinity symbol is so rare. They were both on the rowing team. Everyone knows that. It's obvious. He was probably Melody's lover!"

Violet hid her triumph as no one had told Jean about the symbol being on a ring let alone her previous claim that the symbol was common. They had her now. Since the men weren't exiting the butler's pantry, they were hoping for a full confession.

"That can't be so," Rita said. "Uncle Malcolm's wife is notoriously a light-sleeper, and he's a very heavy snorer. When the yard asked her about it, she told them there was no question Malcom had spent every night in the bed he belonged in."

"But the money, if you were lost, his boys would probably inherit," Jean said.

"There's a motive," Violet said with that same soft, sweet voice, "for Malcom certainly as far as Rita goes. If the shooter had tried to kill her, then Malcom's children may well have inherited, and Rita tells me that he's never liked her. What doesn't make sense is to try to scare her by seeming to almost kill her. Surely you see?"

"I don't see!" Jean said, stomping. "Malcom is the one. I am *sure* of it. He killed that foolish, money-grubbing child, Melody, and then turned his attention to Rita! My goodness, it's a miracle Rita survived!"

Violet didn't hold back then. "Why would he pay to have her almost killed? Especially since he was aware that Melody and Philip were using—" Violet glanced about and then whispered, "Contraceptive methods. No one was in any danger of having a child or changing the fate his children likely faced of inheriting, with Rita being an old-maid and Melody and Philip avoiding children."

"They were *what?*" Jean demanded. "Those—I—I don't understand."

"There are ways, you know, to prevent pregnancies if one has the right connections," Violet whispered. "I've looked into them myself. Given that Malcolm didn't need to worry about an heir from Melody and he wasn't trying to kill Rita, why would he attack them both? He gains nothing. So close together? It would have been far easier and wiser to get rid of the wife and then leave Rita out of it."

"His children will inherit," Jean said lamely.

"Not while Rita lives. She's young yet."

"But she doesn't want to marry. He doesn't really need to worry about her children."

"His children would be grown then. Surely he doesn't want to watch them struggle only to inherit before they die. No, he'd have killed her too, if he were the killer, but he wasn't. It was Mr. Russell. The poor man. No doubt he'll hang. Killing his pretty, young wife. She'll be made the innocent victim manipulated by an older man. A child taken advantage of and then—"

"No, no," Jean moaned.

"Perhaps instead of hanging, they'll shoot him. Do they use firing squads? I think that would be better. A shot from someone who doesn't know they shot you in comparison to feeling your body slowly expired from lack of air, hanging desperately, legs kicking, knowing you were going to die. Knowing you killed your wife. Maybe both wives…"

Jean's mouth had dropped, and she was shaking her head over and over again.

"The poor man," Violet said. "I feel sorry for him, murderer that he is."

"There's no evidence. He didn't do it. He wouldn't."

Rita cut in then, flatly stating, "The ring, the waiter who was arrested for delivering altered drinks. They'll have him testify that he looks like the man who paid him in the club."

"It was *Malcolm*," Jean shrieked. "*MALCOLM!* Of course they look alike. They're brothers. The ring, the similar looks, the attempt on Rita. Malcolm!"

"Has an alibi," Violet said. "Mr. Russell poisoned his wife. They'll probably even make an argument that he killed his first wife. The symptoms are similar to those of poisoning. Perhaps they'll exhume the body and see if they can find proof in her corpse. You know they can tell things like that now. From fingernails and hair and such. Even more so as Rita's mother went from healthy to gone so quickly."

"It does seem like he could have poisoned Mother too," Rita said coldly. She wasn't acting anymore, but Jean was too panicked to notice.

Violet ground in the pain when she said, "I'm sorry, Jean. It must hurt to know the person you care about, love even, will die a horrible death. He'll probably be abused in prison, linger on until everyone he knows and loves is aware of what he did. His crimes will be on display for the world to see and he'll die a painful, torturous, ignominious death."

"That can't happen," Jean whispered. "That can't happen. He's a good man. A loving man. He loved Harriet. He probably even loved that whore, Melody."

"It's inevitable."

"But he didn't do it," Jean moaned. "He didn't."

"The only way he'll be saved," Violet said clearly and evenly, "is if the true murderer confesses."

Jean met Violet's gaze and the two of them stared at each other, each knowing what the other knew. Jean slowly closed her eyes, hiding those brilliant, beautiful orbs. How easy it would be, Violet thought, if all killers looked like monsters.

"How did you know?" Jean whispered.

"It was obvious when we stepped back and looked at all the pieces. If you hadn't cheeky with the attempt on Rita, you might have succeeded in not being found. The murders of the two wives were so far apart no one would have realized you killed your sister."

"Rita needed to stay," Jean said, glancing at the girl. "Gallivanting about the world like her mother. Leaving behind those who loved her. Philip would have let her go back on her adventures, and we'd be left without our girl." Her expression was pleading, but Rita turned away from her.

Jean stiffened and when she spoke, it was with violence. "Harriet deserved to die. The whore deserved to die. Neither of them deserved the life they had. The life they took from me! I met him first, you know. Philip? I met him first and Harriet stepped in and stole him, dragging him around the world, never giving him a home, never giving him a son. He was mine. He was always mine."

The door to the butler's pantry opened and a sick-looking Mr. Russell stepped into the room, followed by Ham and Jack. Ham took hold of Jean's arm. "Did you have anything to say to the man who you destroyed not once, but twice?"

Jean looked at Philip, tears filling her eyes, lips trembling as she whispered hoarsely, "You were supposed to be mine. You were always supposed to be mine."

"I was always Harriet's," he replied. "I never would have married you. I never would have wanted you. With Harriet or without, you were nothing to me."

He could not have destroyed Jean Albright any more effectively if he'd been trying. The sheer honest truth had her collapsing in Ham's arms, and the poor man had to carry her out to the waiting constables.

CHAPTER 21

"Is it over?" Denny asked when Violet and Jack walked into the parlor, arm in arm.

Violet took off her cloche and coat and handed them to Hargreaves. Jack followed Violet's move, handing over his coat and hat. He collapsed onto the Chesterfield, and Violet curled into his side, even pulling up her feet onto the sofa. Jack's were propped on the ottoman.

"You look like death," Lila said. "I would offer you something, but we're mere chaperones."

Jack shook his head. Violet closed her eyes. "It was awful. Rita and I trapped her with her love for Mr. Russell. She confessed in the end to both murders. Rita and Mr. Russell fell apart."

"Will Rita be all right?" Lila asked.

"Eventually," Violet said, "but her aunt—"

Jack nodded against Violet. "That woman was crazy. She'd been harboring a fantasy that if Russell hadn't met her sister he'd have fallen for her. It was as if someone had stolen her soulmate. She never realized or even imagined that he had never been interested in her."

"The more I hear of this story, the more I worry over your sister," Denny told Lila, entirely unbothered by what the other two had experienced.

"Maria isn't in love with you, my lad."

"Yes, I know," Denny countered, "but she is mad, darling."

Lila didn't bother to answer. She propped up her own feet and closed her eyes, ready to collapse along with Jack and Violet, when the door to the parlor swung open and Lady Eleanor demanded, "*WHAT* is this?"

Violet didn't sit up, which seemed to send her stepmother into a rage.

"Violet Carlyle, quit molesting that man this instant!"

Violet laughed in reply, cracking her eyelids as she asked, "Why are you here?"

"To discuss moving the wedding to June. It's more fashionable then."

"No."

"I've already made the changes," Lady Eleanor announced snidely. "It's done."

"I suggest you reconsider what you've done," Violet told her. "Jack and I are getting married in April—"

"The changes are made," Lady Eleanor declared.

"Or now," Violet finished, yawning. "We'll elope. I've discovered sleeping in Jack's arms is quite the thing. I don't intend on sleeping alone again." Jack had become as tense as a rock beneath Violet, so she sat up. "You have your options. Let us know if we need to elope or if you'll return things, all the things, to how I wanted them."

Lady Eleanor's mouth had dropped open and she was clutching her throat, her mouth opening and closing. "You...you...loose, idiotic girl. You could end up with child! From a policeman!"

Before Jack could react to the insult and Denny could do more than pop a chocolate into his mouth with a breathy "Oh-ho!" Violet stood. She crossed to her stepmother, took her by the arm, and dragged her from the parlor, explaining as she went. "Having Jack's children is part of the plan. We'll be married in April. Adjust one more thing about my wedding, and I will pull in Father."

"You foolish child. Do you think I won't?"

"Please," Violet said, "do." She opened the door, bodily shoved her stepmother out, and said, "Don't come back here without an appointment. Hargreaves," Violet ordered, ensuring that her stepmother could hear. "We are not at-home to Lady Eleanor unless you hear otherwise."

"Yes, m'lady," he said.

"We've had a hard day," Violet told him, ignoring the sputtering woman behind her. "I know Cook is excellent, but I want Italian food without leaving the house."

"Yes, my lady," Hargreaves said.

"And cake. Chocolate of course."

"Of course," he said, lips twitching even though the rest of his expression was smooth and even.

"Wonderful." Violet shut the front door on her still-sputtering stepmother.

When Violet returned to the hall, she found herself kissed within an inch of her life. The second Jack let her up, Denny picked Violet up and spun her in a circle, telling her that she had given him the gift of a lifetime.

Lila, on the other hand, said dryly, "Long overdue."

"Indeed." Violet and Jack said together.

Violet gave him another kiss for leaving handling Lady Eleanor to her. When she leaned back, she whispered, "Is that other matter taken care of?"

He pressed a kiss to her forehead and another to the top of her head before he whispered, "Our cellar is in order. Our house nearly so."

"What more could I wish?" She tangled their fingers together and turned to their friends.

"There's nothing more one could wish," Denny replied, "beyond love, friendship, chocolate cake, and perhaps a good nap."

The End

Hullo, my friends, I have so much gratitude for you reading my books. Almost as wonderful as giving me a chance are reviews, and indie folks, like myself, need them desperately! If you wouldn't mind, I would be so grateful for a review.

THE SEQUEL TO THIS BOOK, *Wedding Vows & Murder*, is available for preorder now.

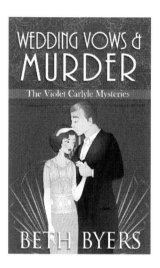

April 1925.

Violet and Jack are finally getting married! The date has been saved, the flowers have been bought, the baker is working on a creation of layers upon layers. With all of the parties and teas to satisfy Violet's stepmother, no one could be more ready for the wedding day to arrive than these two.

When, however, Vi and Jack find a body at one of the pre-wedding parties, they expect their wedding plans to be a little askew. Only the victim is someone they both despised. Now Violet and Jack must solve the murder before their joyful day is ruined. Will they be able to solve the crime, say their vows, and get on with their lives? Or is their happily ever after ruined?

. . .

IF YOU ENJOY mysteries with a historical twist, scroll to the end for a sample of my new mystery series, The Poison Ink Mysteries. The first book, Death by The Book is available now.

July 1936

WHEN GEORGETTE DOROTHY MARSH'S dividends fall along with the banks, she decides to write a book. Her only hope is to bring her account out of overdraft and possibly buy some hens. The problem is that she has so little imagination she uses her neighbors for inspiration.

She little expects anyone to realize what she's done. So when *Chronicles of Harper's Bend* becomes a bestseller, her neighbors are questing to find out just who this "Joe Johns" is and punish him.

Things escalate beyond what anyone would imagine when one of her prominent characters turns up dead. It seems that the fictional end Georgette had written for the character spurred a real-life murder. Now to find the killer before it is discovered who the author is and she becomes the next victim.

. . .

IF YOU WANT BOOK UPDATES, you could follow me on Facebook by clicking here.

Cookies & Catastrophe

(found in the Christmas boxset, The Three Carols of Cozy Christmas Murder)

Poison & Pie

Double Mocha Murder

Cinnamon Rolls & Cyanide

Tea & Temptation

Donuts & Danger

Scones & Scandal

Lemonade & Loathing

Wedding Cake & Woe

Honeymoons & Honeydew

The Pumpkin Problem

The Inept Witches Mysteries

(co-written with Auburn Seal)

Inconvenient Murder

Moonlight Murder

Bewitched Murder

Presidium Vignettes (with Rue Hallow)

Prague Murder

Paris Murder

Murder By Degrees

CHAPTER ONE OF DEATH BY THE BOOK

A NEW HISTORICAL MYSTERY SERIES

GEORGETTE MARSH

Georgette Dorothy Marsh stared at the statement from her bank with a dawning horror. The dividends had been falling, but this...this wasn't livable. She bit down on the inside of her lip and swallowed frantically. *What was she going to do?* Tears were burning in the back of her eyes, and her heart was racing frantically.

There wasn't enough for—for—anything. Not for cream for her tea or resoling her shoes or firewood for the winter. Georgette glanced out the window, remembered it was spring, and realized that something must be done.

Something, but *what?*

"Miss?" Eunice said from the doorway, "the tea at Mrs. Wilkes is this afternoon. You asked me to remind you."

Georgette nodded, frantically trying to hide her tears from her maid, but the servant had known Georgette since the day of her birth, caring for her from her infancy to the current day.

"What has happened?"

"The...the dividends," Georgette breathed. She didn't have enough air to speak clearly. "The dividends. It's not enough."

Eunice's head cocked as she examined her mistress and then she said, "Something must be done."

"But what?" Georgette asked, biting down on her lip again. *Hard.*

CHARLES AARON

"Uncle?"

Charles Aaron glanced up from the stack of papers on his desk at his nephew some weeks after Georgette Marsh had written her book in a fury of desperation. It was Robert Aaron who had discovered the book, and it was Charles Aaron who would give it life.

Robert had been working at Aaron & Luther Publishing House for a year before Georgette's book appeared in the mail, and he got that thrill of excitement every time he found a book that had a touch of brilliance. It was the very feeling that had Charles himself pursuing a career in publishing and eventually creating his own firm.

It didn't seem to matter that Charles had his long history of discovering authors and their books. Familiarity had most definitely *not* led to contempt. He had learned that some of the books he found would speak only to him. Often, however, some he loved would become best sellers. With the best sellers, Charles felt he was sharing a delightful secret with the world. There was magic in discovering a new writer. A contagious sort of magic that had infected Robert. There was nothing that Charles enjoyed more than hearing someone recommend a book he'd published to another.

"You've found something?"

Robert shrugged, but he also handed the manuscript over a smile right on the edge of his lips and shining eyes that flicked to the manuscript over and over again. "Yes, I think so." He wasn't confident enough yet to feel certain, but Charles had noticed for some time that Robert was getting closer and closer to no longer needing anyone to guide him.

"I'll look it over soon."

It was the end of the day and Charles had a headache building behind his eyes. He always did on the days when he had to deal with the bestseller Thomas Spencer. He was too successful for his own good and expected any publishing company to bend entirely to his will.

Robert watched Charles load the manuscript into his satchel, bouncing just a little before he pulled back and cleared his throat. The boy—man, Charles supposed—smoothed his suit, flashed a grin, and left the office. Leaving for the day wasn't a bad plan. He took his satchel and—as usual—had dinner at his club before retiring to a corner of the room with an overstuffed armchair, an Old-Fashioned, and his pipe.

Charles glanced around the club, noting the other regulars. Most of them were bachelors who found it easier to eat at the club than to employ a cook. Every once in a while there was a family man who'd escaped the house for an evening with the gents, but for the most part —it was bachelors like himself.

When Charles opened the neat pages of 'Joseph Jones's *The Chronicles of Harper's Bend*, he intended to read only a small portion of the book. To get a feel for what Robert had seen and perhaps determine whether it was worth a more thorough look. After a few pages, Charles decided upon just a few more. A few more pages after that, and he left his club to return home and finish the book by his own fire.

It might have been summer, but they were also in the middle of a ferocious storm. Charles preferred the crackle of fire wherever possible when he read, as well as a good cup of tea. There was no question that the book was well done. There was no question that Charles would be contacting the author and making an offer on the book. *The Chronicles of Harper's Bend* was, in fact, so captivating, he couldn't quite decide whether Joseph Jones was mocking the small towns of England or immortalizing them.

Either way, it was quietly sarcastic and so true to the little village that raised Charles Aaron that he felt he might turn the page and discover the old woman who'd lived next door to his parents or the vicar of the church he'd attended as a boy. Charles felt as though he knew the people stepping off the pages.

Yes, Charles thought, yes. This one, he thought, *this* would be a best seller. Charles could feel it in his bones. He tapped out his pipe into the ashtray. This would be one of those books he looked back on with pride at having been the first to know that Joseph Jones was the next big thing. Despite the lateness of the hour, Charles approached his bedroom with an energized delight. A letter would be going out to Joseph Jones in the morning.

GEORGETTE MARSH

It was on the very night that Charles read the *Chronicles* that Miss Georgette Dorothy Marsh paced, once again, in front of her fireplace. The wind whipped through the town of Bard's Crook sending a flurry of leaves swirling around the graves in the small churchyard and then shooing them down to a small lane off of High Street where the elderly Mrs. Henry Parker had been awake for some time. She had woken worried over her granddaughter who was recovering too slowly from the measles.

The wind rushed through the cottages at the end of the lane, causing the gate at the Wilkes house to rattle. Dr. Wilkes and his wife were curled up together in their bed sharing warmth in the face of the changing weather. A couple much in love, snuggling into their beds on a windy evening was a joy for them both.

The leaves settled into a pile in the corner of the picket fence right at the very last cottage on that lane of Miss Georgette Dorothy Marsh. Throughout most of Bard's Crook, people were sleeping. Their hot water bottles were at the ends of their beds, their blankets were piled high, and they went to bed prepared for another day. The unseasonable chill had more than one household enjoying a warm cup of milk at bedtime, though not Miss Marsh's economizing household.

Miss Marsh, unlike the others, was not asleep. She didn't have a fire as she was quite at the end of her income and every adjustment must be made. If she were going to be honest with herself, and she very much didn't want to be—she was past the end of her income. Her account had become overdraft, her dividends had dried up, and it might be time to recognize that her last-ditch effort of writing a book about her neighbors had not been successful.

"Miss Georgie," Eunice said, "I can hear you. You'll catch something dreadful if you don't sleep." The sound of muttering chased Georgie, who had little doubt Eunice was complaining about catching something dreadful herself.

"I'm sorry, Eunice," Georgie called. "I—" Georgie opened the door to her bedroom and faced the woman. She had worked for Mr. and Mrs. Marsh when Georgie had been born and in all the years of loss and change, Eunice had never left Georgie. Even now when the economies made them both uncomfortable. "Perhaps—"

"It'll be all right in the end, Miss Georgie. Now to bed with you."

Georgette did not, however, go to bed. Instead, she pulled out her pen and paper and listed all of the things she might do to further economize. They had a kitchen garden already. They did their own mending and did not buy new clothes. They had one hen and were considering adding more to sell the eggs, though Georgette had to recognize that she rather feared chickens. It was their eyes. Those beady, cold eyes.

Georgie shivered and refused to further consider hens. Perhaps she could tutor someone? She thought about those she knew and realized that no one in Bard's Crook would hire the quiet Georgette Dorothy Marsh to influence their children. The village's wallflower and cipher? Hardly a legitimate option for any caring parent. Georgette was all too aware of what her neighbors thought of her. She rose again, pacing more quietly as she considered and rejected her options.

Georgie paced until quite late and then sat down with her pen and paper and wondered if she should try again with her writing. Something else. Something with more imagination. She had felt she had little imagination when she'd begun the story but she'd quite been filled with it by the end of her book.

When she'd started *The Chronicles of Harper's Bend,* she had been more desperate than desirous of a career in writing. Once again, she recognized that she must do something and she wasn't well-suited to anything but writing. There were no typist jobs in Bard's Crook, no secretarial work. The time when rich men paid for companions for their wives or elderly mothers was over, and the whole of the world was struggling to survive, Georgette included.

She'd thought of going to London for work, but if she left her snug little cottage, she'd have to pay for lodging elsewhere. Georgie sighed into her palm and then went to bed. There was little else to do at that moment. Something, however, must be done.

If you enjoyed this sample, click here for the rest.

Printed in Great Britain
by Amazon

61343265R00090